APOPHALLATION SKETCHES:
A THEATER OF AFFECTIVE EXTREMES
AN ANTI-NOVEL

j/j hastain

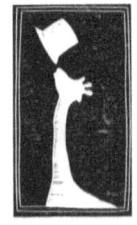

MADHAT PRESS
ASHEVILLE, NORTH CAROLINA

MadHat Press
MadHat Incorporated
PO Box 8364, Asheville, NC 28814

The Library of Congress has assigned
this edition a Control Number of
2016911396

ISBN 978-1-941196-18-2 (paperback)

Text by j/j hastain
Cover design by Marc Vincenz

www.madhat-press.com

First Printing

APOPHALLATION SKETCHES:
A THEATER OF AFFECTIVE EXTREMES

Acknowledgements

Thanks to tt for edits assistance and also for his own work with sketches projects over the years. The parallel of our work in sketch-form has resulted in many revelations. Thanks to Julie Combest. Thanks to Priestess of Ceremonial Arts Program (affiliated with the Starhouse Temple) where a study of Priestess "Chakra Autobiography" takes place. Thanks to MadHat Press, Jonathan Penton, F. J. Bergmann, Michelle Watson and Marc Vincenz for support in bringing this work into published form. Thanks to my Beloved, T, for edits and emotional support with this work.

Note

Compared with the status quo or a norm, many times our body or sensations set us apart as *extreme*. Status quos and norms are basal: not elaborate middles, not ecstasies or elations. The surface is not a valid representation of what goes on (or could) below or above it. The surface is not enough for vision or body.

As forms capable of riding our feeling, we are *embodied extremes* to someone else's (or an era's) societal status or state. Perhaps, then, it is sometimes the case our best choice is to embody accuracies as reason and a way to reach further *into* extremity. We seek beyond attributed or inherited basis and while we leave it behind we understand the base's limit. From that understanding we extend, we sculpt. Flowers bloom brightly through basis and break its limit. Bacteria-rich hydrothermal waters spill forcefully upward through the surface from below, coloring, enriching perspective.

Hermaphroditic terrestrial slugs are born with the organs of both sexes. By their nature they are extremes that differ from other slugs; they switch and change. Hermaphroditic slugs elaborate one another's physiology and pheromone overlap and by doing so they bring one another's genders into the forefront of interaction. Courtship is this.

For these gastropod mollusks, courtship involves assessment and then bodily response. They push each other, first, and then further: further together than they ever could go while apart. They dance into decision. After discerning the aggressor, they collaborate a tightening. Each snail's rather large penis wraps spirally around, into and through its mate. There are times, after the passion of their courtship, the slugs are physically unable to separate. They are so intrinsically connected, now, it seems they might remain this way forever: unified, inseparable.

Then suddenly one slug gnaws off its partner's or its own penis. I imagine this decision involves much less assessment: made in an instant, without remorse. That act is *apophallation*: take a gulp of ephemeral air, then chomp down, amputate your lover's (or your own) dick. Doing so makes inventive amalgamations a necessity. To bite off the dick of your lover after copulation induces sublime drama without threat of the loss of courtship. As extremes embodying our own extremity, we do what must be done.

A replacement organ does not, ever, grow in that organ's place, and due to its removal, the sexual function of the slug is now fixed: without penis. The bite is violent, but it is a violence which pushes the form that was into potential unexpected flourish. Does this slug's gender stay vast and flexible as it deals with its new aspects, the altered qualities of its genitals? In the theater of sensual extremes, the body morphing and adapting is the *body-extreme*. When already that far out there is no attempted return. Instead, there is continued trajectory into flame, into pus. Source is secondary to endurance. We are no longer on the fringe; we are the fringe, moving through references and names, reaching for what of the body could lead into more body.

This book is a first for me: in it I feel obsessed with actual human figures (and other animals) and the actual edges of their (our) lives. I am intrigued by the places in us that terrify and at the same time lift us. These places are fodder for modern myths.

Modern myths need to be made; it feels only appropriate to me that these myths be made by the actualities of our extremes. A contemporary book of modern myths deals in the languages of people's visceral shades, fallibilities, flailings, destitutions, passions, erotics, and even substitutions. As this book is an active un-othering of what has otherwise been othered, there is never anything else for this book to be but beautifully tragic. This is the activism of inhabiting the brim of a world. Here, our embodiments are poethics. We dwell in loads, in yielding.

Herein, pronouns feel entirely up for grabs to me: we, you, me, he, she, it, they, xe, etc. This is also a very new sensation for me, as some of my previous projects were actually about radically renovating pronouns: subverting pronoun norms for underdog or not-yet-invented pronouns. How thoroughly our pronouns assist us in investigations of the accuracies of extremes is relevant. Where are they bridges? Where do they fall short? We, existing, are modern space in need of ourselves as modern myths. Our pronouns (or our refusals of them or forcible demand regarding how they need to change in order to accommodate us) can support our hidden meanings. A place of hidden meanings is not necessarily cryptic. Herein we increase strides, add extremity to extremes, excel by tacit and tactic.

Like our friends the model mollusks, we chew into each other, and find a way through. Sometimes we chew new versions of ourselves out of each other. It's a long-winded chew with a lush snap at the tip of its contrail.

Table of Contents

j/j hastain

VISCERA IN THE FORM OF TIDES

Before you get here, as I wait, I can't help but think there is no way that you will ever get here in enough time. The thought of you comes in waves. Need for weight can crenellate the flesh. It can leave unnerving, inverted gaps: swells. I can feel the flourish of bruises and marks between my legs even though I have not yet been able to open them to you. Do you know how long I have been waiting for this? I wonder whether or not you will use the window. I have left it open for you. I need the gusts that move through it: addicted to night's grease.

I bet you didn't notice me the first time I saw you. You were bent over that car with your back turned toward me, your hands shoved into its guts: obtuse engine made smooth by personified insertion. I noticed how you were bending in relation to the car: not like a typical straight man. You were a little more curve: a fist loosening after the squirming body has slowed. I could see so much on you, in you; I could see the other men to whom you have been a lover.

Image and visions turn desire into swooning loom.

My teeth feel rusty when I imagine. The things I need are resonant resin: tighten the cuff, wrap the encrusted leather above and below my tan line. When you finally get here our bodies won't be distances or distractions anymore. They will be tangential improvisation. They will find a way to fit.

I feel you in me before you are even here, and the rubies in your phantom weight feel clean.

CORE CHORD

The implication is that it has to have been dry enough during that period of time, for it to have felt like a dry spell; aridity as the loss of one thing can also be the perpetuation of another.

Need leads to hallucinations. Longing brings out unforeseen nurture of another. Nature threads a woman into poses intended to assist her in surpassing her own need's brink. Here, a woman is a wealth: a core chord colliding with context. It seems that there is no way for her to get enough rain anymore: insatiable, far from level-headed. Rain makes roves of green outside her window, and the more she identifies as a *woman*, the more she feels connected to Terra. Terra makes her a seer screaming into her own visions. "I know now why Eve refused to leave this place."

During the periods in which no water is present, oil is released by the plants. Emanating oils are absorbed by entities and kept there, within them: rocks and clay patches preserve the succor. What hard key could unlock the meta-senses within this meniscus? Holding factors are willing to comply. They just need provocation: an abrupt nudge. Rain increases: gentle then hard, hardly able to stop itself. The gutters puddle over; the grasses soak. A woman weeps at the precipice of an open window that she chooses to leave open as the water splashes onto her bare, scratched and tightly tucked legs.

She stares into a picture frame that holds a picture of a woman standing in what looks like a ghost town. Dust and tumbleweeds abound. Her tears are so consistent that they seem to be conspiring with the water falling onto the window, then through it. The crack over the framed woman's face is splitting, gaining surface area as she holds it. There is tension here, radiant gradation.

It is the death of certain microbes that makes that unique

smell, and the smell permeates her room, her stories. There are some smells that you can taste. As you push the beets repeatedly into your mouth while slicing them for your upcoming meal, geosmin leaks. You are inundated. This makes you feel, in a moment, as if you now know something that you have been missing all of your life.

Petrichor could only ever occur *after*: one intensity (drought) can be precursor to another intensity (slake) and that interchange changes your life.

ATHENA AND A MAN

Before he pulls his hands out from where they are currently buried in the moist ground, he pauses. His mustache quivers. His back sweats through his thinning shirt in the hardy sun. Sweat makes his wrinkles more pronounced. Nothing in this grove is frail, least of all his heart, least of all this ancient tree. He and the tree are both drought and disease resistant. They have remained here with each other for such a long time. There is something special about them. Calling fire near, they have proven that fire is an element incapable of causing them injury.

He has been kneeling at the base of the olive tree of Vouves for as long as he can remember. He has no memory now of being a romping boy, waddling his way through his father's olive groves. For him it has only ever been this: many sides of a Greek symbol: so many life-giving sides.

When travelers stop at the monument with intent to absorb it, he is there, his body entangled in its expressiveness, almost visually inseparable from the roots of the tree. He is a sword of protection, a silver flash and a red cape. He feels himself as a lover here, though technically he is chaste: has never been with a lover in the flesh.

He does not often think of it in this way, but his behavior, his lifetime, is a form of heroism. That is why Athena adulates him with this stamina-tree, so long-producing. He senses that he is amid a permanent anointing. He often sees Athena in the slow-moving sap, in the messages that unroll like a scroll along the burls of the tree. When he sees her, he stares into her like a child seeping upward, reaching toward stars. She gave him this yearning; she implanted desire inside of him. Therefore it is only through her, through this devotion to her ancient gift to men, that he can hope for satiation.

4

The thought of Athena's spear makes his body lurch; the boughs of the tree froth. He visualizes Athena's spear penetrating the ground of Crete where he is so prostrate. When he sees her spear penetrate, he gets hard. When he is facing the tree he does not try to hide it. He is sure the tree relates to this feeling. How else could it be so fecund and long-producing? However, when travelers near this monument, he brings one hand up from where it was resting with the roots below ground: does this to hide his arousal from those who will probably not understand it.

He sides with ancient Greek law on this: he would punish any man who tried to harm an olive tree. His protection exceeds mortal mission. When at the edges of his sensation, he shifts his shoulders slightly to change his position to add a little bit of relief to his stance. As he does this, his thinning shirt tears: outbreath exudes honor and exhaustion. He knows Athena provides him sensory thresholds like this one for a reason. His clothes are fraying, his body decays. At each threshold he beckons himself to stay longer with, go further with.

Is he ever permitted that thudding permeation of a human death? Yes, many years later.

On the day of his passing, his blood is replaced with it: olive-oil tears. Voyeurs, young boys, stare on from behind a sodden chaos of boughs. What they see of the moment is different than what he sees. For him, Athena is above him, wrapping him in her sturdy, brazen arms. Athena's voice is moist. It sticks to the tops of his eyelids while he is closing them. To the young and chaste boys, the old man looks like he's caught: weeps as he dunks himself backward into a vat of olive oil without holding his nose. They see on him, when he puts himself down into it, that he does not plan on coming back up for air.

This was his wish all along, to be bathed in this way: baptized by the supernatural strength of her sweat-like oil on the day of his death.

THE PROPHET EZEKIEL SPINNING HIS WHEELS VERSUS A SHAMAN SPINNING WITHIN THE WHEELS' INHERENT DESIGN

When YHWH advanced into Ezekiel in the form of penetration, the four wings of the chariot became instantly erect and bloodshot, then fell directly into limpness: violated prey shot by the gibbering hunter. The four live animals (man included) that were previously sprawled beneath the bronze base of the chariot, in servitude to it, shook until their vestments fizzled off of them.

The enforced baring of beasts does not make them feel respectable; animals don't like to have their hair removed. Hair is a part of the body of a beast for a reason: it protects. How can beasts be expected to behave in the manner in which they were previously commanded when the commander takes identity away from them? This is the threshold where chaos ensues. This is battle: the rebellion of the ruled. As he attempts to walk away, the man's feet suddenly dematerialize from beneath him.

How are we to serve when the appearance of the divine in a shapely form reverts our evolutions and advancements? How am I to ever walk the lonely miles of the vale of bones and schisms if the very feet on which I would walk have been taken from me? I am not a miracle worker. I can't walk many miles on these stumps, and even if I tried, then the rising tide of the dead might flash through the desert as a flood: drown me in my effort.

Frankly, projections of a harlot over my homeland hurt my feelings. They do not enable me to offer the best parts of my vision to the work at hand. Couldn't YHWH have just given me a little tenderness? The caress of a mother would do. A prophet is, after all, a version of a human. Keep in mind that my nuances are apteral. If my wife suddenly croaked after divine pronunciation that this would occur, then I would be hard-pressed to not shake my fist at the once-dry sky: teeth clenched as the water engorges. The water is now up to my thighs.

Ezekiel is a hamster, spinning his wheels in a graphic design that is in fact not rotating with him. Imagine the fatigue: around and around in the inside of a stilled, prismatic wheel. You could pass by many lifetimes like that, staring into the starry pupils that froth on the rims, sole witness to the baring of the teeth and those terrifying eyes.

When I learned to inaugurate merge, I knew approximation as a valid method of worship. Approximations of the divine fatten wonder. I prefer approximation because it just might be an approach that the divine and I could share in. If we both approximate, will the hue be diverse enough to hold us both? Will it enable equality rather than keeping only one of us in our place?

An apocalyptic soothsayer prefers I spin with the thing meant to spin. I spin over towing the line. Compliance only gets you so far in a meadow that no longer bears anything green. Even the grass looks brittle here. Green's bones are too exposed for existence to not feel eerie. I suppose that eerie has become a way of life: fractional organic by which I must now live.

FATTY PHANTASMAGORIA

These dolls are doling it out: a-more-often-than-not kind of articulation, aggressiveness. A doll that is moving is a metaphysical motif.

Every time they possess her, she feels relieved that they are in motion again. Whenever they stop, it is as if too much space is suddenly within her. Her migraines come back. She beats her fists against her own head and moans as the memories of her past lovers come in and overpopulate.

When her therapist asks her how she knows she is an obsessive, she points to this fact: she just can't keep her hands off them. It is as if they were meant for *her*. Sometimes they are light, sometimes dark, but they are always full, polished gleam. The first time she ran her hands along the intrigue, the hills and valleys of a mannequin's form, she was a small child. Hands to form, she froze in the store. All other sounds went mute. There were only fingertips and then there were whole hands and whole body pressing against. So this was what it was to belong. "I never feel that with my mother," she thought.

When the hard hand hit her, she found out that her mother had been yelling at her: demanding that she obey. Until the moment of brutal impact she was somewhere else, with them. "You didn't hear how everything else went quiet?"—Young child, there, swearing to her mother that she did not hear her mother's demands.

"Everything was certainly not quiet, little girl. Everyone in the store was staring at me. They could all hear me. What's wrong with you? You made me look like a fool. I know you were doing it on purpose. Don't you dare think that my hand on your ass won't happen again the next time you disobey."

Over the years the lectures continue: some from family, some from her lovers. In her joy, she really feels nothing but their bodies as smooth soothes meant for her. She sees their genitals as elucidating junk (no matter the gender of the mannequin). Her hands are heartthrobs on the knobby dick, on the implication of labial folds. Don't even get her started on the perfectly rounded tits.

In her dreams she constantly resuscitates them. They are here to be *hers*, to be saved. By rubbing them with all of her might, she is able to turn a smoothed arm into a human arm with musculature: an arm to wrap around her, an arm that will never hit. She sees herself leave hickeys on them. Of all of the animal-mannequin forms, she likes the obese mannequins the best: "More to love," she nods.

If you see her standing behind a mannequin and it seems to you that she is peeking out as if she were playing a game of cat and mouse with you, don't misunderstand it as having anything to do with you. She would prefer that you not come over to her, that you not ask her what she is doing. She most longs for privacy in public space. She is passionate and busy in the mannequin spectrum, where she never need remove her hands from those stout, rotund shapes.

When she is in the field with them, everything else is a quiet jism of light.

DEVOTIONS TO DANTE: DIVINATIONS OF A NAMELESS SAINT BY SKEW

It might have been the last day of their lives, or maybe it was the first. Perhaps it was both, happening at once: simultaneity, an atonal moan, an abysmal anti-brevity. The lovers had been returning to Santa Croce for years. Even though Dante's body was not actually buried there, they felt compelled to flagellate in front of his memorial.

"The body only gets you so far," they pronounce as they nod in unison. They agree that there are many things in need of being praised: his life, his name, all of his allusions. He is their sobriquet. They will embody him actively. To do so is only natural, they think; they relate to the feeling of ongoing exile, too.

Some flexibilities are postponed by context. Other flexibilities are inborn, amplified by context and must be lived out. It is the particle-flexibility in the lovers' prostrate that is a sense of self for them. On their knees, by their devotion, they find ways to push each other's bodies even further into flush: forms collaboratively inducing ever more leniency for the sake of the most dramatic, for inimitable love.

In the duration while they have been attending him, they continue to return to the exact same place in the church: on top of the worn-down, horizontal pronouncement. A figural representation of the saint long buried deep beneath the floor of the church has been flattened by tourists who walk over it without much notice. Foot placed right there to try and get the perfect picture.

Dante never performs for tourists attempting to take his photo. Don't they know that? Can't they feel it? The lovers shake their heads in tempo with each other; their tears fall at equal pace. They know that the tourists never pause to consider what saint's sculpted visage they are wearing down with the weight of their position. Tourists just step and step: the sharp points of their shoes wearing away a dead saint's savory details, the only livelihood it has left.

This is how features can be unintentionally robbed from the sacred vestments. The lovers' forms, stretched out over the almost-featureless saint, are indicative of how the actual bodies of practitioners can protect against discrepancies in belief about what the human position is for.

UNCANNY RUSTING IN BOROBUDUR

During the many centuries when the Borobudur stupas were submerged beneath jungle growth and ash, there is no doubt that the Buddha statues within them were resting. It was not until the bell-shaped coverings were unearthed from the weight that had previously kept the resting Buddhas in a state of calm that the great Buddhas began to rust. Unveiling them turned them into restive crests, exposed them. Now they fidget with preoccupation concerning their allegiances. The great stones are disturbed.

Things can be done in order to ensure that your threshold aligns with the threshold of the other beings with whom you are traveling. This is the definitive chivalry of sharing a path.

Access to the sun and to a streaming drip will rust the third eye of any stone shape. Said in legend to be situated between twin Earth elements, it makes sense that so much rain fell over them. The villagers believe it because it is happening to them, too: drought on all sides of them, even while a steady stream pours. It is the rain that is unique: fecundity between flames, between flays. What remains mysterious is how the rain manages to fall (as if directed to do so) only onto the third eyes of the protuberant Buddhas. Somehow the Buddhas are together in this slough. Everywhere else is dry. Green is frying.

Wide baths seem displaced: even though locals have placed them in the jungle in an effort to collect water, the water continues to drip solely onto that point on each disturbed stone head. Resonances of the dinging drips can be heard from miles away: bony tones attempting to elaborate on a form that is becoming brittle in only one place. Is this a revelation? Is it a realization?

When the third eyes of the Buddhas eventually break, will that be the needed shift to alter what has previously been? Will votive candles be lit by villagers? Placed within the enigmatic

13

third eyes of the Buddhas, now smashed in after being made so susceptible? When those flames are lit within, will the rains then finally be un-reined and willing to spread across an expanse of environment for a larger and more inclusive span of nourishment again?

ABIOGENETIC MITOCHONDRIA

"Is this *the* garden? I thought it would be, um … greener."

Large, inky eye then large, ink-covered arm bursts the curve, wraps around yet another shimmering, upward-facing chute. The surrounding environment is desert-like, is the color of wheat: not exactly dead-dry, but a middle-tone kind of dry. Wheat color juxtaposed against glimmering glass makes the glass stand out even more than it would have, had it had no contour.

The glass castle had been being dug up for eons. Figure after figure had embodied mortality, had passed by the entirety of its wholeness in an effort at engaging a part of its wholeness, wholly. As soon as a portion of the castle insinuated that it was completely revealed, a whole other under-area would be found by another digging figure somewhere else. It proceeded this way: fingers trickling along smoothness to reveal and then heights of elation articulated, only to find the need to reveal so much more.

The chutes of the glass castle are cone-shaped; they have a hole at the place where the cone would come to a point if it came to a point, but these cones do not: no *come* and no *points*, only shivering shells spewing a hissing form of mist from hints of tips. The desert grays as it stays.

The Earth: suppressed quixotic in need of many releases. We sashay the channel in a glass sash. It is possible to meet enigma by foretelling reach; reach is always carnal. As women, in the damage-industry of patriarchal inheritances, we pretty much only have phantom limbs. Therefore, if we implant ourselves as each chute is dug up, exposed to light, which increases contextual reflection, it is possible for us to see ourselves divulging what of us might be filled up: turned into fulfillment, human flesh.

The still-unseen base of an impossible glass castle long buried is full of bloody human organs. Many of them are still bleeding, quivering every now and again in the dark as they wait. Women see ourselves reflected in the uncanny spasms. We see ourselves as nature in a manic relationship to engendering more nature.

TRANS PLANT

dedicated to Coy Mathis

On the same early summer days when most Colorado farmers were panicking, cursing as they chopped into the thistles that they perceived to be threats to their crops, she was skipping through her own melodies, emboldened by the joy of her body and her context finally aligning. Her swaying skirt matched the color of her hair: dense fuchsia. She liked that her hair was the same color as the thistle blossoms in the field where she was making music.

Thistles had grown in her yard since she was a small child, during the time when her parents were still mistaking her for a little boy. It was so hard when she did not have words. She tried, then, to show her family what she needed with her body, but that showing often came out as an unmistakable rage. Her family did not understand her then. See her pained grimace distorting her pretty face: grimace at remembering how hard it had once been.

She picks thistles while she sings. She has never minded the slight prick into her fingers when pulling them from the plant stalks; she understands beauty that has more than one aspect to it. "Like me," she says to herself, delighting, "facets." She is proud at this word that she has just learned in school. She likes to turn the word over in her mouth while in the stall in the girl's bathroom, now that she is allowed to go in there again. She can't wait to talk to her dad about it. To say *facets*, forever, until it feels rounded.

In the field, she releases the feral inclination of seeds. Seeds are meant for dispersal. Identities that move are prone to ritual forms of spreading; ritual is inborn to formulas that can't help but flower. It is the coy and clever bees that make the flowers cum; they are nervy and nourishing, they are life-force attending tenderly. It is ultimately the curious and convincing bees (and not the penetrations of a man who was once a boy) that are responsible for wild fecundities.

Investigate and invest in your wild fecundity as it becomes infinite. How does doing so alert your form? Investigate and invest in, regardless of those who might threaten to cut you down. People often misperceive nature; that is a weakness of humans. You don't have to forgive them. It might just be that that particular someone knows no other way than to misunderstand, as they call a flourishing, fuchsia-producing plant a weed.

SHE

A woman is writing in her diary about her confusion. She feels so lost without the part in question: her organ that she knows she has had so many times in planar form, even though it is not here in planar form in this life. Dysphoria pushing her through synthesis, she tries to resound.

"Is my vagina really my dick turned inside out inside of me? Is my vagina my dick in a resting state within? If so, then it provides me the full power within to perform ceremonial merits in the form of the phallus. I need cock to feel fulfilled and I am cock-identified."

Visualizing her vagina as a cave in which many lifetimes' relics can be stored.

Visualizing her vagina as a leather satchel holding bracken and oddly erotic bones.

"If you have an inside-out dick, at least you can't rape someone with it. And I guess it is not even technically possible to rape yourself. "

She palpably proceeds with the parable she is unintentionally building out of the rubble in her babble.

URN

He had been a sanitation engineer for many years. Sure, the smells were intense, but it was good money. He loved his wife and the work was worth it to him. He enjoyed cool mornings when he was transporting leaves; the leaves would float and spill out of the top of his sealed truck. He always considered how poetic it was when dried leaves were released during spring: a lucid conjunction.

He and his wife had been trying to get pregnant since just after they got married. Because she asked him to do so, he wed her before he really wanted to be married: the things you do to be able to fuck the woman you love. He knew he could wait no longer at second base. His feelings would flood his heart, then his balls, and he was sick of jacking off at home alone after he dropped his future wife off at her house. So she was old-school; he could live with that.

When he saw her in her white dress, with that birdcage in her hair, he felt like he had an eagle flying in his throat. How could it be that she had never been as beautiful as she was now? He felt his feet lifting off of the ground ever so slightly. He wondered if his male friends could see his joy.

When they lost their baby for the third time, he felt numb. He had tried to talk with his wife so much about this that even his words were making him sore. Maybe his sperm was fucked up? The doctor said that there was no noticeable problem with her body, so maybe it was his? He took all of this so personally. His doubt made it harder for him to hold his wife.

On that morning, when he saw the doll's hand sticking out of the bag, about to be smashed under the weight of the metal of his truck, he jumped to stop the continuous compactor, grasped at the lever just in time. By the time he had her unwound from the refuse, one of her eyes had fallen out. He loved her all the more for having only one eye when he lifted her up like a father with his favorite child: lovingly into the light.

Something happened when he held his finding. The doll softened in his arms and seemed to him to be like a little expressive urn for the lost pregnancies. Daddy's little girl smelled like garbage, so he knew he could not take her home. Besides, what would his wife think of him holding a dirty doll so near to his heart? He could keep her in his locker at work. His locker was in the back and he could slip in and out of the locker room without anyone asking him about daddy's little girl.

The emotions are a desperate and delicate wash, like collecting tears in pillow cases and trying to transport them. He went on for months this way, until he and his wife were finally pregnant again. "I guess I could return her to the landfill now," he thought to himself. On the day that he planned to do it, he could not get her to separate from his hand. Was she holding on for dear life?

Any subject that you remain haunted by continues to be a valid one.

Blood Falling From the Jowls

She had gone far beyond the border. A mother having her cubs out somewhere in the periphery (and hiding them from all interested animals) is a visionary. She scopes out what dips in the dirt might provide shelter. She pulls at the bushes with her teeth in order to make more tangle in them. The desert is an environment where protection does not come so much from the land as from an animal's own vigor in relation to the land.

When she first spots the large male lions running toward her pride, she is aroused. They are a temptation, but only in that first instant: short-term temptation. She does not know whether to run from her cubs and warn her pride or to remain there with her cubs, tucked away, possibly safe. What would be the purpose of going to the periphery for her offspring if there were no pride to return to? Part of the reason you ever go is to feel what it feels like to come back.

What if the impending coalition breaks the flow of their tribe-estrus by tearing apart the females of her pride? The females have fallen into something whole, together in their bodies. They have been able to defend their pride against intruders by reading each other's minds until now. Which role is hers? If she returns to her pride, these cubs' bones will be crushed in the mouths of now-approaching, power-hungry males.

Her cubs are all females: three, to be precise. The pride is their future home. They will not be kicked out of the pride to fend for themselves as male cubs eventually are. It is at this point that, shaking, she has made her choice. She takes each of her cubs' whole heads affectionately into her mouth as if to warn them: "Don't follow me when I go. I will do everything I can to come back. Take care of each other while I am gone."

She squeezes their skulls one at a time: a synonym for a

thorough and passionate mother's hug. When she gets to the last cub, she is perhaps a bit too vigorous. Her heart is beating hard, she is sweating and her paws are shaking. The cub squeals a bit in her surrounding strength. She does not know that she has crushed its head until she sees blood dripping from her mouth onto the arid red dirt. Her gut clenches and she lurches backward. She is afraid that her babies might notice, but the other cubs are so delirious from the pressure of her recent hug of them that they are on their backs cooing, on the brink of sleep.

A moment is a fleeting duration: probably not the best time to make a decision that might impact the memories of your living young. Regardless, she considers waste and the possible trauma of leaving her dead cub's body behind. Brashly, she grabs the dead cub in her mouth.

She will stare into its eyes in her memory as she runs toward her pride. She will remember how lovingly it looked at her, in all of its defenselessness. She will do this as she eats her dead child.

From 440 Hz Back to 432 Hz

Pitch has been used to socialize. Modern music's impression differs from sound's capacity to heal. We are bruised by the difference, the dissonance. To have changed nature (music in 432 Hz tuning) into something out of balance with it (music in 440 Hz tuning) has enabled sound control where sound ceremony may have been its actual cosmic design.

Standing in front of the orchestra, preparing to play this or that concerto, she cued the clarinet to play a concert A. This was not unlike any other day. She felt a flutter in her eyes: a flutter that flashed, then left a small gap. The orchestras for which she had been Concertmaster had never concerned themselves with the vibrational distance between 440 Hz and 432 Hz. Although she could definitely tell the difference between either case of A, there was not much she could do about changing that plight. Enforcement of the 440 Hz had been doing its damage for as far back as she could remember: long before she was born. When her parents played music to her in the womb, thinking they were doing her a service, they probably unknowingly drenched her in a damaging vibration.

What do you expect of her? Is she to throw a fit, tear at her hair, disassemble her violin on the spot there in front of all of the players whose thoughts are on what they are going to have for dinner or how sore their backs are, totally unaware of the damage of the dis (the changes from 432 to 440) as she is brutalized by the vibrational difference? It's a distance she feels, really. Is she to lash out at the design-flaw in the Conductor's hand as he shakes his head negatively, implying that the clarinet's concert A is out of tune with the 440 tuner in his hand?

No. In order to be able to play with the group, she has to align herself with both versions of the A.

As a person with perfect pitch, she hears the differences in the frequencies by feeling; if she is to not go crazy due to that difference, then she has to find ways to work with it. Those ways of working would later cause her to develop a relationship with the cyborg for working with hybrids, mixes. This would make her realize that instead of feeling perpetually disturbed by the dis (and having to live with a small gap), she could raise the dynamic of dissonance in all of the music of her life: do this by her own will. She could turn this inheritance into a thorough crack in her psyche.

The visions she got from cracking the 440 wide open were versions that were worth something to her now, as she began to try, and find. Having eventually left the orchestra, she is now invested in the other side of the other side and whether or not that place is capable of returning her to nature in a form that differs from a circle.

An eight-vibration difference per second has a dramatic effect on human consciousness. In 440, overtones leak or shred, lose their pull on the third eye. Vibrations which do not align with nature cause the release of stress hormones: the flight reaction in herd behavior. When you hear classical music tuned to 440, do you inexplicably feel like running out the door as retort? When you feel the ground begin to shake while the orchestra is tuning, do you want to pull your own eyelashes out? Do you weep at a high point in the composition for what seems like no reason, and wonder if you are being controlled by someone hiding behind the curtain, like the Wizard of Oz? Perhaps all of these are your body's natural reaction to pitch having been unnaturally altered. If you feel compelled to escape from a scene that you are in, then perhaps you need to re-tune the concert A of that context. It is your right to do so.

She is continually retuning now. It is possible to progress by sympathetic congruence, to do so for coherences of energy, to support and engender the most natural spin. As she grows through works within this subliminal devotion, she remembers that as a child she heard the 440 Hz tuning more often than she even heard her mother say "I love you."

She decides that being human now is more complicated than it was for the first humans on Earth. She is a cyborg becoming a human woman. It is for this reason that, in process, she commits to giving herself a lot of breathing room and access to some grace.

BLOOD

It began when she was a child. The first time a child got a paper cut: a little bit of red leakage, then a lot of reaction from the adjacent adult. When you are a child any adjacent adult is an adjoining adult, a demanding point refusing to be sparse to your experiences. You just can't seem to get your own space to investigate and make your own decisions about your body, about how your body is contiguous to—and impacting or garnering—the world.

As a teenager she began to make a spectacle of herself: would leave the blood from the cuts accidentally made while shaving her legs, running down them like paint or extra-bright stretch marks. She let the red pool at her feet, between her toes, stain her skin and remain there throughout the day until it crusted. Even when it was cold outside she wore short shorts to show it.

She liked her step-mother nearly choking on her granola as she strolled past her and closed the door before faux-mother could comment. When people's glances turned into inquisitive stares at her, she felt she had succeeded at something very important to her. They were trying to solve her in a truncated timeframe: that mereness wherein they were walking by her along the street. Time in passing is never enough to truly figure someone else out. Anyway, she didn't want to be figured out. She wanted shock.

When she finally moved out of her step-parents' house, she would always keep white sheets on her bed while menstruating, collect her menstrual clots in rags and wipe them into her hair and along her body. A performance amplifies a stage. She kept her bed blushing with the reds of her body and the white cum of her lovers. She needed to see the extent of the pulp in order for her to rest in it. For her, it was how the sheets were stained that made it her bed.

Pupils seize in their sockets as they engorge on innards' pigment. This is how the insides move outside of the body: how and why. Blood constantly makes its way in an effort at contextualizing flesh, exteriors. Status quo does not have her fooled. Blood is not just some internal thing, meant to be left there or humiliated as something terrible when it is expressed, when it expresses itself. Have you ever thought of your cut as in need of expressing something to you? She thinks about this all the time.

Whenever she is feeling lonely she looks to her blood to remind her that it is impossible for her to ever be abandoned or alone. Her blood is right there with her in each plump pump. That is a fact.

ORPHAN BLACK HOLE?

Is a child lodged in the pressured clamp of the birth canal and fourteen hours belabored an erogenous silhouette of a nomadic black hole?

The child is twenty days overdue. The mother's push is all desperation at this point. Having long exceeded the postures of grace and duty, her sweat cascades from her pores like mouthfuls of waterfall. Even the tops of her shoulders are sweating. She screams and she tears. Her asshole is turned inside out from all of the shoving; her veins are fattening below her skin. Body here, is unintentional engorgement and it is taking her: taking. At the edges to which this sensation is bringing her, is she slipping away into cosmic water? Is she reverting to the child that she once was, resting in a sloshing womb of pain, a valid, vital abyss?

Astronomers have been studying galactic graphs: merge-outlines. Colossal convergences suggest that, depending on their size (which intensifies their influence), certain massive black holes are nomadic. This nomadism, however, could only ever be the result of energy-heave. The previous directionality of a black hole's travels is immediately reversed upon impact with another supermassive. The queue of magnetic gelatin prior to impact detonates when the two touch, and from that moment onward, propulsion is immanent.

The mother and the child are both supermassive in the context of the scale that they share. They are trying to touch each other; they are striving. After more tumultuous hours, the baby is finally cut from the body during a Cesarean birth. Its head is cone-shaped; it takes many days of the mother holding the baby and gently dropping water onto the infant's head for it to smooth into a rounded shape.

Whether by pushing until the form is turned inside out with

love, or driven by energy until the form collides, illuminating by
conjunction, a hole in contour with another hole is art.

SKIRTS AT A BAR

It was blatantly obvious that the two women were lovers. You could practically hear them fussing and chanting, now, what they had been saying to each other earlier in bed: "Lover!"

"Oh lover!"

As the light in their bedroom changed, their thrusts inevitably increased. Thrusting can be profoundly inclusive, even if the bar you are dancing in together later is not. They did not hesitate to make themselves noticed: skirts intermingling while they danced in the beer-stench, seemingly oblivious, staring at only each other. So many mean miens, such disapproving stares.

The surrounding men and their skinny girlfriends shot looks like darts, yet the lovers chose out of experience of those as violences capable of being inflicted on them. They had other things on their minds: each other's bodies, the palpable smell of one another's rare sexes on each other's hands and mouths. The lovers kept instinctively stepping over the splits in the wooden floor. This was step as leap; they were not going to let anything separate them. They were going to be right here. It is possible to exercise bizarre agencies for the sake of accuracy. Identity-exertions are a must.

Sometimes you can see people's secrets as winged, floating over them. From the moment they stepped into the bar they saw only each other until they were surprised, sensory-addicted to that man. He was quite skinny. His hair was very thin and his clothes were torn. He was the cause of many other men and women averting their eyes. As he danced, his arms flailed around like oranges dropped into long socks; they were Slinkys. When the music in the bar changed, turning tempos, the man remained in the middle of the dance floor, gyrating, oblivious to the hard stares of others.

The lovers were hooked. They could not help but look on this man as a miracle. Was he blissed-out on some invisible form of Shakti, a resonance with more in it than his body knew how to deal with? Would divine energy discharge from within him and ricochet outward, blowing forcefully on the troubling grimaces of these surrounding men and women?

The lovers kissed, embraced, and with sea-eyes, nodded; they felt good about sitting down together to rest. This man was their totem tonight. This man meant something for their future: *him*.

HENNA

Otic oddities in an outcropping where forceful winds catch.

There is only one figure in the totality of the image. That figure is wearing a dark, velvet cape, wind violently whipping it, but not lifting it enough to reveal any details about the figure's form. Are there bodily distinctions here? Is there a pronoun? It is beginning to snow outside. Snow catches on the trajectory.

When the view accelerates, vantage shifts. It becomes possible to see that the figure's hands are embedded in a large, cone-shaped pile of sienna-colored powder. The pile is at least two times as tall and three times as wide as the figure. Viewed from above, it looks as if the figure's hands have either dematerialized at the wrists, or as though the pile is swallowing hands by sucking them into it. Sensate-magnetisms bring forth predator or prey. Prey on the palpable pheromone-key. Pray and pay homage at the base of a physical phantom, an ongoing French kiss.

From appendages embedded, ink starts to climb up the figure's skin. By the time it reaches the shoulders, the falling snow has stilled. Inner weather dominates: what an aurora relies on. View attempts to track the traveling ink. The volition of the view is longing to retain this enigma that is so much like sleeping on a wooden pillow.

Quiet and oil. Oil the color of splinters pours over. The figure feels the pricks of sharp shapes in their closed eyes. Tears fall from closed eyes onto the large sienna pile. Curvaceous marks of salt and water are like henna marks in a materiality meant to be inked, not received.

Oily rune rakes the lungs for an ever more kingly ilk.

He Honestly Kneads This

For t thilleman

Sure, he had had a shitty childhood, had left his parents' home before he turned eighteen and hitchhiked across the country imagining Jack Kerouac to be with him in person, as he gripped a worn-out version of Kerouac's *On the Road*. Jack was the only book he owned; Jack was his only friend. He would repeat his favorite quote out loud to the air as a stretching quaff. He believed it to assist the landscape in its changes: "The only people for me are the mad ones, the ones who are mad to live, mad to talk, mad to be saved, desirous of everything at the same time." He loved the grumbling truck beds, how it felt as if they were alive and generous, gifts of female width, massaging a gilded vibration into his back. He later realized that those vibrations of his late teenage years were the beginning of his love of touch as an initiatory form of healing.

Now, so many years later, he is homeless. Some folks just get the shit end of the stick. In and out of various menial jobs, dealing with bosses who know nothing about gaining and practicing skills that increase the clandestine tremors in the body and urge the body toward catharsis: each spot of lack, so very fatiguing. These had caused him to drink too much during a few years of his life; they caused him to lash out at the person above him in the chain of command.

It has taken him a while to get where he is, but he has done his part so that no one at his current job—including his clients—know about his past, about where he sleeps at night. He has had this job, and been receiving shining reviews, for almost a year now. Whoever said you can't be homeless and proficient at your job was wrong. He had not had a drop of liquor for nearly two years; he was proving himself. This fact made him proud. "So sometimes you have to lie while you are jumping through hoops. Lying on your résumé is like Jack's kind of mad: nothing like life-giving madness to stabilize a man."

Every day he wakes up early enough to be at the local massage parlor fifteen minutes before his shift starts. By showering and shaving at the YMCA he can look very professional, regardless of the fact that he may have had to walk a few miles in the snow to buy some canned beans with a pop-top for dinner the night before. The more he works with clients, the more he realizes that he cannot believe in a destiny that is blind to his own desires. So if he wants to pass as very together—as not-homeless—then he certainly can.

After all, whose business is what his home life is like, anyway? No one's. As long as his clients feel release, feel the threaded gold coming out of his hands into their muscles, then as far as he is concerned that is all they need to know.

At the shelter, after the long days, he sits back into the frayed blanket on his cot and thinks about each client. He makes personal notes on the nuances of their bodies: tries to learn from touch. "That woman was challenging to work with. She was so skinny! I could tell that she has not been eating. It is hard to get into the muscles of someone who is making themselves sick due to lack. Oh, and that other woman with the big-muscled legs: she was not lukewarm in the limelight! What a relief. She must have had many massages before. She was so comfortable in her skin." These were a kind of nourishment to him. He could eat them on nights of no food.

Sometimes his reflections actually replaced physical hunger in his body: made him able to disassociate from his surroundings in the shelter completely. "Hmm: that last massage of the day was intriguing. Was that a woman or a man?" Even with them naked on the table, it was impossible to tell. Quick internal adjustment—a little more politically correct: "Not that I was trying to figure it out or anything ... that's not my job. Healing them, regardless of who they are, is. They kept letting me go deeper and deeper. That is probably the highest pain threshold I have ever worked with on a client!"

He passes through his clients in his mind and body like falling leaves, like items that he has for a few moments before losing them to another moment. He suddenly recalls the time he intentionally hid his wallet in the top of a very tall tree, which, when he left it there, had full leaf-coverage. The contents of his wallet were scant: a maxed-out credit card and a picture of his daughter. These would certainly be of no benefit to others, he thought, but he still felt the need to protect his relationship to his memory of his daughter by putting it as high up as was possible in a tree. When he got back to the place where he had hidden it, as an above-ground kind of temporary burial, all of the leaves on the tree had fallen off, and the wallet was nowhere to be found.

THERAPY

"Do you have a preference on the gender of the therapist?"

Pause so drastic that the pause itself could be breathing. Pause on the part of the person who has made this call, hoping to receive some hands-on therapy to help with the pulled muscle in their groin after rough sex last weekend. Pause in the body of a person who does not identify as a woman or a man only, a person who knows that when they are being asked about the "gender" of the therapist, the person asking them this question does not know that what they are in fact referring to is born-sex differentiation. The person being asked this question wonders if something should be said about gender versus gen sex. Saying something is decided against. This call was about the strained muscle; it wasn't supposed to be a damn lesson. Xe teaches this stuff all day to the students anyway, and xe gets sick of having to be the one who is teaching all the time.

"I want the best therapist that you have on staff."

Many hours in the day have passed since the call and xe is on the warm table. Xe has just given the therapist permission to bruise xem. "Go as deep as you can. Depth is the only way I can think to counter deep pain." Sometimes xe has visions. It was a vision of the body being emancipated by the pronoun (as opposed to it being boxed in or held down by it) that first brought xem to *xir* in the first place. "Xir": pronounced like *fur*, which is different than pronouncing it like *her*.

Tussles in the Grease on the Train Car Floors

Can you paint the surface of a river if the river is not solid? Is it possible to make a liquid thing solid without it having to pass through a *trans*?

Transubstantiation emphasizes that more than one truth exists at one time: the cracker so white that it almost glows is a form of winter; it is a body-buzz on the tongue. Whiskey is a form of wine and wine is the blood of a genteel savior turning and turning in the stomach, calling to you from within.

These teens have been on the road together for almost a year now. All three of them decided to leave evangelism together. Their collaborated choice took courage. They don't talk about it, but courage, privately, makes each of their cocks hard.

None of them pine over the ferociousness of their mother's negatively nodding head: God! That went on for so long! They don't fixate on what was or what should be. They never really believed in *should*, anyway. In the firmness of their bodies, the boys of summer are finding new ways to proceed: strong smells, arousals, un-brushed teeth, tussles in the grease on the train car floors.

Thin legs dangle as they sit on the open edge between doors. The teens are side by side, passing the jug back and forth and swigging. What they speak of while so much green and wheat-colored country passes them by is not scriptural; speak matters much less than what they see. In seeing it they feel it: So this is the world that we've been missing.

Because they came from the same church and the same kind of upbringing, they agree about many things without even having to state them. They are a three-part mutation, and having actively left their mothers behind, now they are nodding. Though invested in transubstantiation as a philosophical prompt in their upbringing, it is not really valuable when you are trying to live by your body rather than by someone else's abstract interpretations of what your body is for.

Food that tastes like food feels like food going down. It makes you full when you are hungry; a bowl could be filled with anything. Perhaps that is all there is to it: no transubstantiation after all, no inner-ringing from a particle-Christ demanding sacrifice of them from within them. Being commanded by an imaginary figure inside of you is a trap, they agree: it is insanity.

At one time, prior to them leaving, they had the guts to actually have the discussion. Looking both ways down the church corridor before bursting past its closed doors, they ditched their classes. They walked together until they reached the wheat field, then sat there in the ripe gilding. As they ran their hands over the softly cutting strands of wheat, a three-part confession took place. "I am attracted to you, too!"

"I have been in love with you since we were kids!"

The conversation that precipitated their departure was a conversion of sorts. They had always thought of Christ as a fantasy lover. It was not that he was a girl to them, but that he was something to enter rather than an ephemeral engineer perpetually entering *them*. They would make themselves blood brothers, then. They would release all the warnings that had been instilled in them by socialization, and would do so in a wheat field, warming each other's virgin asses as reverie.

Pictorial swerves are elating the potential for a shared picture to sustain them. Three wild boys are leftovers from lightning dreaming of itself. Behind closed eyes, ravenous light continues to crack through the dark during the moment that they have closed themselves to what they finally understand to be artificial light.

HOT SLIT

Gertrude Stein had visited many same-sex couples in that cave. It was a well-known fact: folks traveled across country for access to it. The managers of the location eventually had to set a limit on how many couples could be in the cave at one time so that each would get what they came for: the textures of her priming attention.

Reflection is a solid that moves; therefore, transmission is assured. What many came to call the *martyr's cross* was obviously apparent to participants when they finally made their way to the back: pool by pool, coolest to hottest. The cross could only be seen in the reflection of the waters of the hottest pool. If you turned your head to gaze up at the stones in an attempt to find it where it supposedly originated, then it disappeared from view. A cross is a shape, and a shape can black out if you look at it the wrong way. Shapes are alive. The martyr's cross is sensitive, prone to fainting. Be careful where and how you use your penetrating look.

Gertrude usually entered the cave when someone was staring into the water below them, head bowed, taking in transitory shape. Slipping in from dark light, Gertrude would hover over the vulva-like strip at the back base of the last pool. Burbling syllables and phonemes would come out at the same time as that firm touch. Hot slit was a point taking place in the shape of a curve, and beyond it, beyond where Gertrude hovered, there was no light or lingering at all.

The smell of burnt coffee and sulfur kept the sex organs of the couples loose while they were being touched and spoken to; you can't be primed by a visitation when you are stiff. The abounding awareness which came to participants during visitation was not exclusive to sex or gender. They all knew this: they were in a constant menstrual cycle below ground. Her menstrual cycle.

While waiting in line for their turn, two young girls who had obviously ridden to the cave with someone old enough to drive were feeding each other bright, crunchy cherries: cherries so crisp that they popped each time one flew from one girl's hand and landed into the other girl's mouth. With a flick of the wrist, compelling fruit is lobbed from one body in need of loosening to another.

Martyr's cross is a message taking place in plashing, hovering form within an ancient cave. Of the many others, a cave is the most whole shape, and a whole shape is worth lifelines upon lifetimes of inquiry.

WEIGHT

Brother and sister are stressing the small scooter. Are they doing this on purpose? Very likely. They know that they are beautiful in this: the force of them altering the suspension of the small vehicle. Their outfits match, slightly.

Her black dress is short and her thick legs are sticking out from under it, bouncing a bit as they move along the road. There is a teal ribbon around the waist of her dress. It is like an exterior vein spilling forth between them. The vein reminds her of Frida Kahlo: all those capillaries capable of being blown by the wind. His belly is dear: just big enough. He is wearing jeans and a black tee shirt and though he presents as masculine, he often ponders nests. His shirt has a teal lining that matches the vein in her dress and he sees it being looped and looped into the materiality of the next by rare, luminous birds.

They are a living inversion, changing time by bouncing with the obtuse. As they weigh down space, they are uplifted by the result: gamut and juice winning out over social pressure, a longevity shared by both psychic and physical lineage.

COMPULSION AND COERCION

Sometimes after waking from a nightmare nothing feels right. Are molding dolls, long suspended from island trees, applicable figures? If so, then how to refer to them collectively? This is the desire to honor; no insult is intended.

Ghosts are always applicable, and they don't like to be offended.

It was believed that the lone inhabitant of the island drowned one evening while running from the ghost-girl who regularly haunted him. He had come to the end of his rope; his nerves were always on edge and no matter how much he begged her, no matter the rituals he performed, the ghost-girl never let up.

Early one afternoon he performed puja in an attempt to show her his feelings. "See, I brought you friends," he said while she stared into him. He pointed upward like a child toward more dangling dolls. He often felt better for a moment when he pinched their cheeks. The dolls' faces never snapped open, revealing horror like the ghost-girl's did. He did not really like the color pink, but he was willing to try anything: pinch a doll's cheek, call dolls the instance of pink that was capable of reaching him out here within the gray and grief that swallowed his days.

Now all that remains are the dolls he once hung as bridges: efforts to tell the ghost-girl that it was not actually his fault that he could see her. He hoped to have some day proven himself, tempered her, let her know that he meant her no harm.

His body floats face-down in the tides: it has been that way for years now, decaying. Scuttling insects cling to the dangling bodies of the decaying dolls, and the ghost-girl seems to have receded.

The dolls swing whether or not there is any wind.

CARRYING

He had been waiting. We all had been waiting in the usual hour-long line that existed on any Friday morning at that post office. There was noticeable tension in the whole group. Feet were fidgeting. Outbreaths were over-accentuated. If it were winter, then expression of emotions would have made fog-like areas appear on the windows: exasperation constructing a place to write a nasty note to one of the three clerks behind the desk.

When he finally made it to the front of the line and the clerk brought the buzzing box out from behind the wall where it was awaiting pick-up, his joy was unmistakable. Tears were in his eyes. It was clear by the firmness of his grip that instead of handing it over, the clerk wanted to keep holding the wooden box: a little afraid and very aroused by what was inside.

When the man who had been waiting jerked his bee box from the clerk's hand you could see it on the clerk's face: he was hurt. He had wanted to feel the buzzing box in his hands forever.

CANNING

She had considered it her sense of place and simultaneously her sense of self since the first time she slid her knife into the skin, then into the flesh. Fruit and vegetables are excitations, even if you are never the one to eat them.

Her eating disorder had been out of control for years. She would hurry home from work in order to be the first one in line at the farmshare; what goodies would arrive today and how could she preserve them? She never considered what she was preserving them for. She certainly was not too concerned with taking more than her share of something. She was not preoccupied with the concept of waste.

Would there be some future date in which she would gorge on the contents of her jars? Probably not: gorging was not in her nature. Were the jars full of jellies and jams, goulashes and salsas her trophies? Were they forms of kills?

When she ran out of places in which to put the full, sealed jars in her home, she began putting them outside: in holding nets in the rivers, in the ever-present shade of old pine trees. She started with the land surrounding her home, within her property. Eventually, even those areas were filled past capacity. There were stacks of jars exhibiting different combinations: shapes and colors galore.

Eventually, she had no choice but to move her jars and their contents out further, beyond the boundaries of her property. She always had anxiety about where to leave them, about who might be fingering them: who and why. She cared about them. She wanted to enable reprieve.

"The contents of jars need to rest."

Whether or not she ever ate them, at least she knew that her dears were alive. She could see on them what they had been through: an enabling bio-violence.

COULROPHOBIA

Not only do I wish you would have taken the mask off sooner, but I wish you had never put it on in the first place. The difference between the way that I know your body and the way that, ever since the first time it happened, I remain unable to recognize your face brings out instinctual abrasiveness in me. I can't help it: phobias gel with other phobias.

Looking back on things, I think I could see it on you the very first time; I could tell you had slept with her. Over your face I saw melted cake frosting caught in fog; your countenance was smeared. I think I waited to confront you about it because I wanted to see if what, of you, had become limp and frightening to me (your face) would return to normal. I mean, who really knew? "Maybe Mercury is in retrograde a little longer that astrologers projected. Maybe I am just imagining things," I said out loud to myself on yet another evening when you should have been home with me and were not.

This was not what I agreed to in "until death do us part." It has to be valid, even cosmically correct, to disempower the thing that most brings out fear in you. I can't be the only one that feels this way. Maybe I can start a support group.

The next time I go to the circus I will bring along buckets full of hose water, water balloons. I might even load my spa in the back of the truck and bring it here. Hell, my husband and I certainly aren't using it together! If I encourage the children at the circus to fight their fears head-on, then maybe the countenance-smearing will not have to happen to them.

It's about time that a new birthright is made clear: children have the right to drown clowns.

Man to Man

Rough, left hand is literal weight over an elegant organ: one which is covered by a tattered piece of cloth. There are these oscillations: not back and forth but through, frothy. Questing the length and width of a natural, horizontally-placed stanchion moves you deeper into wilderness. The strength in it: flip of the wrist then the flippant wrist being grabbed firmly.

A feminine Jesus is showing us a little leg. Surrounded by summoning angels but not being summoned by them, this Jesus expresses through the sharpened nail in the smooth right hand. Marks are being made on the inner thigh. A phantasm bleeding? Deifying masochisms are pristine replacements of typically human, glib machismos.

Is this how a savior asks to be called by a different pronoun than what was attributed, than what Mother called them? Is this the power by which a real man, unbound from social mores, leads so many other beautiful, sweating men out into the forest to be with?

You wonder if Jesus is hiding magnets under those flowing clothes. You peer, straining to find the origin of this draw over you.

Then you get it. This Jesus is the magnet.

POST-COITAL TRISTESSE

The room is bare, but the sheets have a high thread count; it is possible to see that fact from the backlit doorway. A single hand in respite points upward, finger against a lax face, a face in repose. This face is more expressive than the clasped hands propped up on their fingers in the lap of the body to the left.

A small wrath can ravage sleep just like a ravenous one can: parallax. Is she fretting among instrument frets, agitated by a vision of an expanding organ made from human pelvic bones? Sure, shapes fit in other shapes: it is part of their nature. But pelvic propaganda, felt in the body after the lover has pulled out, causes disagreements, the feeling of imbalance.

Is that a concrete slab beneath both of them? Could it be that by some strange proclivity they share emotional scale regardless of the fact that one is so much larger than the other in the view? Even though they have just fought?

She doesn't understand why he is still talking, why he still obviously doesn't get it. She just feels inexplicably vulnerable after sex. She has told him this before.

WAR

There is blood in the river but the river is not dead. A battle has just taken place here and everything throbs red, rhythmic.

Non-human animals have been traveling to find this place. They have been following their noses, their senses. They are nearing here, and they are this place's after-the-fact. They make themselves a part of it by taking it up as their own, inserting themselves into a place's memories. Places themselves are exerting their bizarre agencies long prior to the arrival of wandering animals. Will animal bodies, falling over in exhaustion as enormous gems, provide poultice for so many human losses at this site? The site of scars?

Make note of what is felt: a blood-washed fern partially full of chlorophyll is also partially straining against exposure of its frame. Bloody-mouthed vultures with tremors in their armor fly down to try to dip their beaks into the carnage of so many carcasses.

Intelligences in carcass caress.

THE SUBLIMINAL THREATS OF SWADHISTHANA

She had decided long ago to actively put her womb into a resting state within her. It was not that she hated her womb or that it posed a gap in her gender (as was with the case with some of her beautiful lovers: her stone butches and her trans men). This was not wishing death on a part of her form, nor was it intentionally dis-easing her relationship to herself as a woman.

She wanted to relate to her womb. She just couldn't do so without activating it in the form of bearing children, and she had decided (based on overpopulation of the planet and the lack of time in her life in which she could raise children well) that she would not bear them at all.

When she explained this to fellow practitioners of Dahn yoga they did not understand. Used to looking at physicality as a place to track symptoms more than as a place of somatic agency, it took time for them to get her pledge: the one in which she regularly slowed the breathing of her womb.

Instead of *womb* being a resonant chamber, full of living potential to birth human offspring, she had turned it into a cave, a place to resound agency (regarding offspring) and to do so as a solitary practitioner.

SLOPE

She is ready: a nonchalant bull's-eye; but she is not actually awaiting him.

It's not that he chooses to be a jerk; he can't actually do anything about this. His body is his personality: gray to darker gray. There is no physical way for him to jack off, so when he is aroused he goes to her. His role regarding her is biologically defined. The cavity in his mouth aches: compels him to lick her clit and anus, stay with her, court her until, nervously, she pees into his mouth. He drinks her pee to test pheromone activity: to see if she is ready for him. What is her excretion indicative of? He asks his question of her body directly: hidden tractions brought to a forefront by physical presence.

Biologically prone to being too aggressive, he is certainly not born to cuddle. He shoves his tract into her and his penis hardens without increasing in size: not much fun for her. Exchange is covert and even though his dick does not engorge, she can feel him there; he has forced himself in. Her tail bends to the side. Her whole body stiffens. He usually only forces himself into her one or two times. Coordinating overlap, he hopes the limits of his physical power don't eventually render him unable to complete his task (he can't stay up on two legs keeping her body in one place, and stiff, for very long).

She feels irritation after he pulls out. She pees again to get the feeling of him, and his excess sperm, out of her. She is caught in this, she feels. Though her body says it is ready, she is also, always, just looking forward to returning to the grass. She likes her neck bent down and loose much more than when everything about her is suddenly turned rigid: her stiffness to meet the stiffness of his frame.

The dramatic slope on the back of his neck catches her

attention. Slopes on the neck are not much different than slopes of grass. As she and the other heifers meander around the fields, it is their relationship to slope (and not his little, always-impending dick) that makes them feel safe.

Black Lung

It had finally managed to make its way out of the hive. Who knew that leaving the hive would ever be a relief for a bee?

Having moved from the depths of where it had spent its whole life (subsumed in the collective buzz), when its body was outside of the hive and solitary, the sun and air-clarity was a surprise. So this was the other side of what it had known. The other bees of the hive had been attacking it for months: nibbling until its hairs, its whole history of softness was gone. As the bee continued to turn black and its abdomen bloated, it knew it had to make its way on its own from there. The most abrupt moment which forced it over the threshold of the hive's lip, occurred on the day when the bee realized it was no longer able to fly. Chronic bee paralysis had pushed this bee over the edge.

Miners, so far within it, fall to their knees in the cave when they finally see them. There are so many crystals: years of atomized compacting. They are gazing into a literal miracle while their own bodily interiors continue to be blackened, forced into collapse by their context. Their lungs have been charred during their work amid the dust. Is it worth this? The human body collapsing from within itself for the small paycheck and this one momentous experience of kneeling before a superhero penchant (as these crystals so obviously are)?

As it dies on a dying aspen tree on a cool day in autumn, the black of the bee's swollen abdomen reflects light.

IN THE THROES OF GMOS

Does it ever come to a point when contamination is immanent? Can what has already impacted be reversed? If pesticides are so culturally normal that without rigorous avoidance of them we eat them daily, then do our bodies build up immunity to them in an effort at protecting us from a future potentially damaging to our physical longevity? Are we turned so inside out by that to which we have been exposed that there is actually no way to prevent further exposure?

He is not sure if it is the cancer that did this to him; he can taste chemicals in everything he eats now. This makes him reluctant to ever eat. He has been dreaming of green blaring into green: hoping for a hero, a Lancelot to appear out of what remains hidden to him, that forest. He is so very skinny; his husband lovingly reminds him of this: points to the thin patch of skin over his protruding ribs.

Is this a visual over-accentuation of Adam's obsession with the rib? Was Adam's obsession with the rib, an obsession with the garden more than it was ever an obsession with Eve or woman? Ribs look a lot like the knotty twigs of old growth trees reaching out beyond. For his body, reaching beyond is reaching toward. On his deathbed, all he wants is some organic zucchini: phallic vegetables from the garden he and his husband hand-tended.

At the moment that he passes, his husband is holding him in his arms. As it happens he sees himself standing in a forest where it looks like ribs are doubling, providing him access to. Are these ribs exterior neural ducts? Can he breathe with his mind now? Is he finally embodying a place in time and a planetary state that make sense to his human cells?

He is open; *open* is alternate to asylum.

CREPUSCULAR SPECIES' STARE

She was telling her mother that she would definitely adapt if her whole life could be one of unchallengeable strength during blue hour.

"It's not even that I hate sunlight," she said. "I just feel myself so free in all of that blue: the between. It's like nothing can get to me there, like I don't have to even remember how abusive all of that felt, how much he hurt me."

She is singing at the local blues bar tonight. It is her regular gig now, since she moved out of the house she and her ex-husband shared. However, it is very irregular that her mother is in attendance. Her mother is Mormon, you see; doesn't drink: is told by her father that she has no place at a bar.

"Why would you even consider going? That isn't avoiding the appearance of evil. What if someone we know sees you?" Dad shoves his perspective into Mom.

"Honey: stop yelling. Why would someone we know be at a bar? Besides, they said she is getting really great reviews. I want to see her perform. I don't have to be doing what everyone else does at a bar in order to be there with her: you know, supporting *our* daughter. She still hasn't recovered from ..." Mother is trying to say something unmentionable and violent out loud. She can't do it. She can't face what has happened over time to her little girl. "Just cut her a little slack."

Crepuscular species' anti-predator adaptations are about maximizing the likelihood of a prey's existence, persistence. Over time, your form changes so that you can avoid being captured. Since the divorce, she has shaved both sides of her head: has a blue-dyed Mohawk. She does not even look feminine anymore, which means that to other potential husbands she does not seem feminine.

Her mother doesn't like this but has decided, for once in her life, to not shove her opinion around like a weapon. It seems like there has been enough shoving lately. Her daughter has been too proximal to danger, and Mother wants to be the bigger man here: bigger than ex-husband and father. Mother being the bigger man is an antidote: syrup in the synapse so that a struggling child does not need to feign.

Thanatosis is really a bad sensation to feel; tell that to the child who has fallen to the ground after taking a drug and being hit by the back door.

Mother rounds the building to try to meet daughter in the alleyway, just in case there are any less-than respectable men there. If Mother sides with daughter, then there will be two of them, and two are less likely to be attacked than one.

Mother never sees daughter come out the door around back. Mother ponders staying a while there until daughter appears, but then realizes Mother is now in the alley alone: no between-blue here, she thinks. She could be preyed upon.

Mother turns and hurries out of the alley.

CHEMTRAILS

It is not possible to know what is pouring out of the backs of jets.
We are either within the jets, reading our magazine, swatting at
our child or we are below the jets, on the ground, looking up
while holding our child's hand and pointing. It is only the air
that knows what is being released from the back of a jet, and it is
only the air that can verify what damage is being done.

Is our weather being manipulated by the government, salt and
silver iodide being mixed with atmosphere to induce more rain?
Are harmful chemicals being poured over our backyards from so
far above us that the source that pours remains anonymous to us?
Are doppelgängers being brewed in the space above our heads?

Evaporating tungsten leads us to face the other end of a light
bulb. The hand that holds the light within the house must hold
with care, or the gummy gem will weep, secrete. If secretion
occurs, then the surrogate will bleed. There will be nothing left
to do but stare at it, stare out the window.

Seen through glass, a large sandstone head sits on a lawn. The
head is drenched in the morning light and air. The head does not
indicate whether or not this figure would be male or female if it
had a body. You can't tell the sex of a shape by staring at a head.
There is the sense that the water moving over the head is stuck
somehow: liquid repeat in replete, the threatening and epicene
center of a prospect, a scene.

STRIDULATION

Stridulation is a form of adoration, really: adulation.

Their volition vibrates as night stretches in toward them. Nature coerces union. Folds don't sing without parts being rubbed against other parts. There are many reasons to make music come from your form: personal being made public, blessing environment with spume.

With their ears on their knees, crickets are listening to and feeling themselves as they perform their lyricisms. Males court females with the quietest of their songs. It makes sense that the sounds, in response to rapid shifts in temperature, would differ from a cricket's articulation of their territory. It is obvious that these would need to differ form a cricket's love noises: ways to interest a female. Perpetuation of chromosomal matter depends on these males not scaring the female away: watch her run away if you shout at her, watch her move closer to you than you thought she would if you coo.

Miracle is: "I project images of myself into matter and matter reaches back toward me: makes these connections." Desire is an unconditional, internal bruise. What better approach to something so dramatic than to make a spectacle of it?

The rumble of subliminal opera becomes a tug, a tagline, an unexpected torrent in the crickets' collective howl.

A Fairy Tale Starting off the Rails and Then Going Further off the Rails

There was a young woman who lived in what seemed to her to be rue: sticky, thick, textural, true. Not sure how she got there, not sure if she belonged, she tried to embody a lastingly strong song. She tried to feel preferences while she waded through, but more often than not she engaged with what she was stuck with—with crude.

One morning she woke to her work the night before: piles and heaps of fabric on the floor. And ducks were many, waddling and stout, all different colors of them, as usual, strewn about. Just as she was unclear how she had arrived in this soup, she did not recall the origin of her obsession: ducks in the basement, ducks manning her roof. "They must be my friends," she thought, soft. Their feathers are sinking in fireplace soot. My boots, they are covered, my boots and my books.

Great pockets hung slack in the tunics, which, when linens were lifted off the floor, were proven. The subject of the previous night's work was impressive, sewn in place of riven. So this was the night-watch: completion of tasks when previous eyes are gone. So this was a way to increase competence, hidden connotations: rights in place of wrongs.

A woman who surprises herself in her seemingly sudden, passionate love of small ducks of any color is obsessively making her own tunics. She makes the pockets noticeably large: maybe even too large by someone else's standard. "Big enough to hold many at once," she thinks. As she says this out loud, the duck in her hand squeaks.

RAPE

There are five (or more) figures under scrutiny. Four of them are back to back. Between where they have been tied together, thin trees jut up, pressing. Green gore: nature's erection targeting the place that each member of a pair's backs touch.

Is this recompense? What happens to these men after they have aged, gone to confession and said their Hail Marys? Made the prompted, wild pronunciations until that small section of the rosary that pertains to their sin feels to them like it has actually become a part of their body?

The four, back to back, detect disgust in Mary's stare. When she peers at them, shaking her head, they can feel her stare as an erection; they are sure that it's coming for them. They do not know that their actions, their lives, going into Mary's third eye are what make that area on her hard. "Don't mistake this for a hard-on." She shakes her head side to side with command. "Nothing about this is proof of arousal."

The four are up to their knees (and the lone single, to his thighs) in the murky water of a flooded forest. Some heads are drooping; others are lifted up to the sky. Each of their eyes is covered with a sash.

He who stands alone is weeping. He is frustrated as he gazes into the history of his own psychological need; he is seeing himself face-to-face right now and he is not impressed by the close-up. He wishes that his father or someone else who could have gotten through to him back then would have let him know that committing rape is so much bigger than what it seems to be in a moment. It's not just having gone a little bit too far.

Rape is like fracking an oracle.

SLOW SAND

After waking from the dream she could still feel the sensation.

The sand that falls from the top of an hourglass into the cone-shape that gathers below it was falling over her clit, endlessly, encouraging inner rumbling. She felt herself as a tremor being initialed by a tool like a tongue: a tool that never spurted into deflation and instead stayed moist, steady. She liked it.

Having long privately considered what it would be like to bat for the other team (actively checking out her lesbian neighbors, having crushes on her female co-workers, masturbating in the privacy of her own home to woman-to-woman porn), this dream made her float by pulling her body up from where it was lying below toward what was pouring over her. This dream might have been the subtle-but-maximum sensation needed in order to push her over the edge.

She had come to relate to being penetrated by a man as being struck inside: losing her air and sinking into quicksand at the same time. Sure, he seems solid, she toys, but as he fucks her she disappears far below herself. Sometimes, when he has been drinking, he overlooks her clit entirely. She feels that when she is down so low, she is submerged in a hollowing abyss with no hope for the natural floatation that occurs when the object sinking into quicksand equals the weight of the displaced water and soil. She can't ever remember a time in which he made her float by pushing her down.

There are innumerable men inhabiting the antechamber of an amphitheater. They are peering over the bars, using their hands to push themselves out further. They want to see what kind of mud-wrestling or woman-on-woman, honey-and-tits thing is going on for them below. They assume they have been invited. They expect ointment to be spread over elk.

When they see that there is nothing below to excite them, no pairs of women to objectify, some of them bugle. They think this will call women to them. They tarry. They wait. Then they strain over the bars again expecting response to their bellowing. The same subject who was below before remains there, even in the wake of their need to objectify. She is one fully clothed woman slowly dropping granules of salty sand, one at a time, from one of her hands into the other. A cave turned inside out means miracle, means crystals on the outside.

"This is bullshit," one bull says out loud as he turns, puts his back to the woman. He and the other men are going to leave, grumbling all the way out of there.

Shipping Noise, Shrapnel

She admitted it: she was obsessed with her daily regime, so many rituals enacted without rest. Photograph after photograph of the bed with only one sheet on it: the bed in various phases of expression, like the waxing and waning of the moon.

Something in her ears felt biologically interrupted. Her hearing? Her equilibrium? Her own sense of balance? Regardless of all of her efforts to find more than one resolution, it was only the light moving in degrees over the rolls in the purplish sheet of her bed just after waking that brought her relief of that interruption. Ritual was a way for her to interrogate interruption by beauty: to invert or divert distance instead of drowning in it.

"The body is the only unconditionally sacred theater," she thought to herself, while gently rubbing her open hand along the sheet: the impressions therein. She tried to remember the weight of her lover as leverage next to her. She felt that remembering safety due to the closeness of her lover would let her connect with the feelings of pods.

She was worried about the sea; she was worried about mass beachings. She was worried about her own hearing loss, how crazy that made her feel. The length of her hair was noticeably in contrast to the forties slip that she wore during these rituals: array of time spent actively. Her necklace dangled like a loophole, a danger, a recap regarding the damage that hard things not native to the sea (fishing gear) can do to groups moving together in unified motion as pods do.

She did not really see her hand (moving over the sheets as a way of making the sheets of motion, indigenous to something), as a penetration or an abstraction: definitely not a hardness. Her hand over the remnants of her lover and her in their bed was the tender caress of the beaked whales that had been reported as beaching themselves most frequently nowadays. No one knows why shipping noise and sonar penetrations affect beaked whales in this way: driving them into an extreme in which they are almost guaranteed to perish.

Her hands clenched as she whispered, "Don't get sand in their blowholes and don't euthanize them. Help them back into the surf where they can listen with their subtleties and attempt to find their way out of the predicament that has been imposed on them. We must, each of us, be given chance after chance." She was holding her ears now and rocking. "If we have resources, then we can be the suppliers of magic, of another best chance."

Pollinating immoderations, the dying, frail whales and she are cosmically for this: consciousness-evolution by vivifications. A savant is a sidereal capacity. She will turn her rocking into music. She will show the photographs of her sheets in the gallery. She will turn the unfair, the deadening, into art.

SADHU

That he is the lone one in the view does not mean that he is intentionally eremitic. He is not trying to prove anything to anyone else by separating himself, he is just separate. His bowl is placed on a stanchion as the snake continues to wrap itself around his free arm. Shiva is always blue, but here and now, Shiva is more-than-blue: morose. Shiva is looting a practitioner's halo.

Does he inadvertently inhale cremation ash as he sits near the Ganges, contemplating smear? The materials with which you work have a way of getting inside of you. Working their way into your veins, they are artful ways of keeping track.

It is possible to be your own source of inspiration. However, to do so requires that you have the alchemical wherewithal to leave yourself, exist outside of one or more of your identities and be accessible to you *by you*. You become the thing you are aspiring to be and you reach it through that.

To devote to complete darkness as a way of eventually finding his way by unforeseen light has located him at the foot of a corpse. In what ways will he use his relations as his altar? As an aghori, his insistence that oppositions are illusions allows him a reason to speak with the passersby. What method to devise for getting and keeping the attention of others? Rows and rows of skulls are lined in front of where he sits on a threadbare mat. The sharing of bones may or may not be an affront to the deceased. Either way, bones remind him of himself.

He is drawing out blood from his own body. He hopes to stain someone. He is cutting off layers of his own skin and trying to show them that, if it is dried, then it is paper: no more need to cut down trees when we have so much body to work with. He hopes that eventually his own skull will be painted with designs, flowers, the secret names.

POST-OP MEETS THE PAIN OF HER PRE

When she and her girlfriend would make out, she could feel them exchanging faces. Sure, it might have been how much of her woman-face she missed until she had it, but she could definitely also feel herself as *her*, then, when she still looked to others at least partly like a *him*.

Her girlfriend had told her many times, "I think you are very sexy as you are. You don't need to change. I like how petite you are, how soft your arm hair is. I am *queer*; I've always been aroused by the between. I love to tangle my hands in your thick, long hair." She worried that when she eventually got the approval from her therapist, and then got her operation, that her girlfriend would be disappointed and would find her less interesting, because, after all, at that point she would (finally) be *less* between.

Agdistis is sprawled within the grip of an enormous armchair. It is only possible to see the small bits of her appendages. There is a tattoo on her right arm, the arm which hangs over the tall side of the chair. The chair is holding her in the needed adjustments. Below the hanging arm there is an oversized pile of fruit peels. The peels do not seem to match the skinless fruit that is being held, loosely, in the palm of her dangling arm. Both of her genitals are flexed, but one feels more right to her, even if the full view of both of them can only be detected by her. She can tell what is right for her body. She looks as if she is about to unintentionally drop the dysphoric fruit.

True to her fear that it would be the case, she and her girlfriend broke up after the operation. She could sense it in her; there was a problem now. She did not understand why her girlfriend could not just project between-ness onto her without making that projection apparent to her. Don't we at least, in part, see what we want to see of others?

Or is it always the case that we are being seen and sought by less primary parts of ourselves? Often, to her own dismay, she saw her previous face in herself. She did not want to see herself as a him *ever* anymore, and yet she still did. She sensed herself as privy to protraction, even possibly as victim to portal. She had had her operation so that she no longer had to writhe when what she saw of herself in the mirror took over how she felt herself to be. What if this never went away? What if she always saw *her* as a sometimes-*him* in herself?

When she decided to cut her hair into a chic but short hairstyle, that choice was not as much about the personal demands of her gender identity as it was about her trying to cut some of her ex-girlfriend out of her. "She always loved my hair," she stated, really feeling the loss of the particular closeness she once had with her ex. Granted, she looked good in this haircut, and she was excited to be going out on a date tonight with a lesbian, but she did still miss her ex.

When will experimental compassion finally be agreed upon as a fleshy and valid genre of body by which we can flesh ourselves out, pursue the cavities and protrusions of our own authenticities? It is in such an experimental compassion that our bodies can be unconditionally shared.

MEDDLING IN THE FORM OF MUDDLING

Instead of toppling the tower, instead of crushing the image of their dream, the book of Genesis emphasizes that God chose simply to muddle their speech. They could keep their arching bricks, but they would lose cohesiveness. To force people in on themselves, to interrupt by tone, seems a surprising and jealous approach for a God. God had shown this jealous face before, but why this time, in this case? Why now? What was there for a God to be concerned about when people worked together to make a name for themselves, a safe culture in which they could thrive, an unbreakable bond?

An envious God reads strength and independence in others as a threat.

It is possible to knit by geography and vision. Etiology depends on our expanding its tendencies to tell, to show reasons. Babel: a great jumbling. Where so much effort was put into the tower, populates of the city wonder on the value of reading each other's minds now that there is such complexity of language, now that there is such disconnect in regard to meaning. They literally trip in the streets. They fall onto their faces while trying to pronounce the differing pronouns. But what does that one mean if this changes? But how far can this one go into change? Confusion is sticky. It makes the ground choppy: the dirt sucks the soles of your sandals while you are trying to walk. Pronouns: profound confoundment.

Reach your cup toward the one who is pouring into it and ask for more. "More." There, simple enough. That is what it has come to now. But what if they could understand you the way they once did? Everything that you said would be taken into account, would be an opportunity to get further in. If it were now, how it was then, you could share: "Tannins. More of what is at the bottom of the barrel. I love the murkiness, the complexity of the taste, even though I hate to feel confused." Explication can bring you nearer to having the specificities of your needs met.

A young tomboy is tired of not understanding her parents. She feels exhausted at having others try and shove her into boxes, simply because they don't understand her. She shoves her knife into the air: one foot forward, then hand forward, flipping the wrist. It is as if the wind gusts are there to be tempted, tempered by her penetration. She is sword-fighting with what it is that comes at her, what she can't control.

In the privacy of her own body, she bows to her gender as some would a garden: that which guarantees food, year after year, without trying to understand anything as pre to the food's appearance. In her own form, her variances are totally clear to her. At least God had not peppered that with confusion.

If God had taken that from her, she might have just killed herself: taken herself away from God.

SOJOURN

It had been happening most intensely for the last year or so: hordes of people traveling hundreds of miles just to let go upon their arrival there. They were making themselves intrinsic to the artfulness of this endeavor. They were letting themselves go by falling. In a manner similar to the artist who had recently begun creating man-made caves, this artist had deliberately placed them in a field where there were no trees: just sky, ancient boulders and flounces of velvet. Before long, hundreds of emotional people were throwing their bare bodies onto the large velvet boulders. The artist had made this place so unique that, as he emphasized could be its potential, the place was calling people in.

For children up until a certain age, a velvet boulder is a velvet boulder and not a metaphor for falling in love or a metaphor for increased vulnerability in an era when environment is becoming too industrial. Ever since Jimmy and his parents had returned from their familial experience of letting-go, he could not stop making them: the noises and the specialized stones. He kept some of them hidden, he rubbed others on his skin: rock after rock with velvet strips glued over them.

His art teachers at school continued shaking their heads. What was cute to them initially had now become an issue with this child's participation in class. By doing what he wanted to be doing and not what he was told, they said, he was interrupting. They were sorry, but they would have to report this to his parents. Head-shaking, finger-wagging. After all, this might be "anti-social" behavior, and everyone (art teachers included) was afraid of that!

Years went by; he aged day by day. Jimmy contemplated. It became more and more obvious to him that not everyone could let themselves fall as a form of letting go. To do so was a choice, and after you did it it oriented you differently than others were oriented. Metaphor was stretching itself out within him.

"It is possible to eat your life as an open tone," he thought, turning his tongue in his mouth. Tone is for testing tastes.

EPHOD

When they performed ceremonial carnage together, they shared a sacred vestment. Their ephod had a spine built into it, and the spine often poked their posture, made them move with one another as they adjusted themselves for the sake of poise. "Poise is where posture meets purpose," they agreed. "Poise is inborn nourishment of potential zenith."

They pined over the spine that alerted them. They spun it in their practice as an ulterior dick, an elegant strap-on that trailed right up the back of the form in which they were each investing. These two feminine males, performing communal body as a form of enlightening gore, knew that they needed an unconditional place from which to root, in which to root. After all, sometimes their own organs were flaccid from exhaustion, overuse or simply mood, and even if they had to move via a loner organ, they wanted the erotic bone on which they leaned together to be one that could be depended on without doubt.

When not performing, they often discussed how the scarlet threading of their article felt most like their personalities within their bodies: reddening ribbons clamped onto, entering, and engendering the ions of a shared face. How is a face being read while it contorts? What is that particular read assisting with? What is it taking away?

They name their parts after pouty jewels. They reach into and into a pocket, sewn into the vestment. The pocket tightens and widens. The contents of the pocket are fingered while they hold so tightly to one another.

A red hat waits in front of them. While performing *each other*, there is not the space within them to wonder if you will leave them a tip. But if you do, then know you will have done something that mattered. They have no other way to pay rent than this, now that both of them have been brave enough to try something else: to stop turning tricks.

ALTERNATES TO DIS

It wasn't really that she needed to get a sex change. She was changing all of the time. Sure, she considered this or that medical intervention when the feelings got to be too much. Sure, she felt as connected to the shape of a phallus as to what a phallus might enter. Who could blame her? There were so many ways to live form right. The more she moved through her feelings and her body, however, the more aroused and driven she was by the idea of rinsing herself of the sensations of displacement, disturbance, and distance by what she could subliminally create: by making empty places full.

Internal architectures, placed by volition, outside of her body, were sites in which she could grow: out of or beyond. "If I am growing in more than one place at once, then, sure, I won't be in control of everything, but I also figure I have a pretty good chance at not being an unintentional ending point by not dying due to the limits that others might have me live by."

She thinks of her father. She can hardly conjure his face from memory anymore: it has been so many years of his disapproval regarding whom she loves, regarding how she presents herself aesthetically. Were his cheek bones hard, rusted? Or was it that his cheeks, when he managed to smile, were soft?

Years pass. She practices.

She is beyond gladdened each time another and then another empty, prosthesis-like glass shape crops up. She sees each of these as essential ways to cross, as abiogenetic agency-allowing units: triangles, soft rectangles, squares becoming orbs. She fills them with pheromones: invented and biological. She fills the glass forms with burned leather, lavender from Tuscany. She swells the glass shapes with discharges: different discharges with different names depending on what this or that elation or loss was like.

She teaches herself to liquefy essential organs in a short-term way so that they can slide into the glass forms and then later pop back into plumpness again.

So many self-realized neutrinos enter and none of them are ever forced out. She is getting familiar with the parts of herself that exceed. Familial expectation, singular narrative, and even the idea of roles and pressures regarding them are losing their grip on her, causing her nearly no distress: almost no calluses at all now.

"Don't console the role," she muses. "Make glass and then meld living things with glass. Make more world to work with."

TRITONE

Even though xe would successfully use them in ways that radically differed from how they could, at times, be used against xem, xe regularly stated that xe would mourn with a craze of the soul if there were no longer mirrors on the planet. Xir gestures have the power to change how xe looks to xemself aesthetically, which is all the more reason for xem to look into xemself over time. Compare three distinct chapters of a life to three whole-tones climbing the invisible steps of each other in hopes of their exertion affecting nature. Nature's expressiveness exposes. It is not only the major second or minor third. Sometimes tone is awkward, dissonant. Dissonance can disclose.

Can smears in form welcome unforeseen light? Is light an ever-after challenge, a place capable of pulling fatigued or lost forms into the forest? A slipknot is being tightened and loosened, spit on, lubricated while it holds. When xe had to get the CT scan due to concerns about xir heart, xe was afraid. "They will focus on the breast that is *actually* my *chest*" xe murmured (not just a glance in the mirror while walking by it, but a blatant stare while allowing the eyes to cross). Xe often shoved xir gaze sideways and into the full moon like this: searching out reflections, the shadowy God with its silver blood, trying to see what is really there in what is looking back at xem: the paradoxical contents of a looking glass.

The backside of the mirror and the underside of xir shadow are the same color: awareness by tritone, the taste of a round thing's edge.

What's Beyond Ally?

What would you do if your little girl dreamt of Natty Gann every night? Is a girl who definitely passed as a boy in the story an appropriate model for your own child? I mean, you are an ally to queer people (you tell yourself this), but what happens when you need to bring all of this nearer than ally could account for? What of your own life must you change to accommodate bringing what you might have only minorly othered in your very most private moments in the past into your own home now as your own?

Encourage a streaming emulation: doing so puts pulse back into the delivery mechanism. It allows the person who you used to habitually call your *little girl* to keep dreaming of the girl-boy's ingenuity and power, to keep dreaming of the girl-boy's success in finding their own missing father. Miracles happen in children's dreams; sometimes they even build their own bridges within them.

Your child is thinking, teaching herself from within the Natty Gann story. Miracles occur on mountain roads just outside of an androgynous child's father's base-camp. Outcroppings are novelties: places for rainwater to fall and to gather, and places where the handsome stubble-face reflected back to her in the water just might stop your sweet child in her tracks long enough that she not miss him in translation again. You decide you will not say negative things about her father (the man of her dreams) anymore. You consider how it must feel to her to have had her daddy leave you, leave her.

Next time she is roughhousing in the kitchen, you decide you will put a space between her and your usual reactions. You start pumping weights in the loft so that you can lift her over your head higher than your neighbors might say a *girl* should be flown. Improvising new levels of intimacy, now that you have simply let yourself, you are surprised how you feel good when you rumple her hair like you would any other boy.

What Shaking Has to Do with Shamans

Voyeuristically viewed by a crowd of clothed people, bare backs are dripping with blood: strange maps of devotion. Maps of devotion are not necessarily maps of encounter.

The shamans flagellate and shake regardless of whether anyone is watching, whether or not they will ever get to meet the God for whom they perform their puja. One of the bare backs' flagellation-marks is the shape of a heart. I imagine his imagination to be heart-shaped too: an ulterior-integral assisting in enactment of divinations, making itself visible to him via his unearthing his own blood by his own hand.

I always feel impact by sound first: screech of tires, visceral timbre and the quiet screams of a body that, just a moment prior, was still in flight. After it has stopped squirming, after it has died, I carefully remove the bird's broken foot. The removed part of an animal squeezed in the hand of the person who is consecrating it adds loops. More cars are pulling over now, watching.

I suppose experimental compassion could look different to a gawker than what it actually is: a tender performance of care regarding when a bird's legs have broken, when its eyes have exploded out of its face like too-ripe berries. I violently shake my body as I burn National Geographic photographs: photographs of poachers who were recently caught with hundreds of de-feathered and crisped songbirds in their trucks.

Breath is the mysterious backbone of every moment. I breathe heavily as I bend in the middle of the road, stopping traffic. I shake with the bird as it passes: it does not have to shake alone.

The shaman's shake is the only panacea. You must shake yourself, and you must shake your neighbors. Too many fucked-up choices are being made in all of the more usual stasis of the quotidian. Don't stop. Don't stop the shaman's shake until something surprising emerges: once-extinct subjects emerging anew as peculiarities on the rise.

Pit Alter   Pit Altar   Pith

Inviting in intuited aliases often results in a moaning moon on every side of the measure.

At an abandoned train station, Ana Mendieta meanders. She is wearing lipstick, which, to anyone who knows her, is strange. She also has her usual beard, the blaring clot-lozenge of her dark pupils, and her power as fringe, embodied. Silueta exudations are a masculine form of nature. She is wearing a dress. That is also a little bit odd, but the fact that it is sodden and stained with mud … well, that fits Ana perfectly.

Is a feminized ghost slinking its body along the railroad tracks that no longer ever get action in the form of traction a thing by which to be inspired? He hopes to move closer to her. He needs recompense. He will try to move slowly enough that he does not scare her off or push her into a sudden Silueta materialization. He's not ready for her to be blatant Earth again, even if forms of blatant Earth are stunning, are ways for green to change places with green and for other colors to show through as the result of that interchange. She must know that he has too many questions for her in her current, shocking and unlikely state for him to push her into anything else that she might also be.

As he nears her, some zombie-like swagger enters her meander. She notices him. She shares the scene with him now. He wonders if she feels obligated. He wonders if he looks like blatant Earth to her. She looks at him with one bleeding eye. He tries to catch himself in it, so that her look might become a stare. Roots drop down. He feels himself swallowed in a swelling legend.

There are obscure and abysmal forms of grace. In the grace of Ana's bleeding eye, a goldfish flops and writhes as it and the liquids of its bowl are being poured out. Beyond that point in her eye, the contents are raked over in an anonymous pit filled with gravel. The goldfish in the pit must have been how she felt in that crepuscular hour when she fell (or was pushed) out of the 34th-floor-balcony window. Neither she nor Greenwich Village would ever be the same.

The Lingam Learns to Linger

There are so many different kinds of orgasms in a woman's body. Some flood upward until the spine spins. Some fold the whole form so forcefully you think the spine might split into two, then four. Others are like ash poured over ash: carnal mixing. And still others invert spill, rearrange the usual crescendos and diminuendos: hanging and falling. Small, red wooden boxes seem to be falling off the wall, but when they near the floor, where it is expected that they will crash, instead they hover a bit, float.

Doors are opening and closing between the walls. Either the walls are wide or the doors are thin: paper-thin. Wind gets caught as a little cachet as the movements are taking place. Are these elliptical doors? Sound is catching and it mirrors Ujjayi pranayama breathing practice. This is how the ocean makes its way into her walls: an engorging purr, a purifying enthrallment by sibilance. The ocean's wooden cavities curve as they accrue so much sensation.

She is blowing up a prolonged prong: a phallus-shaped balloon. Sound makes its way to freedom by her following the long trail of a fray. She has been blowing and letting the air out but never allowing the balloon to go completely limp. She feels a vibration in her body and follows that vibration to an interpretation. As other Taoists practice it, she wants the most severe version: *coitus conservatus*, her lover controlling his ejaculation entirely and never letting any of his essence be lost. With her lover, she wants to free the lingam by limen.

She perceives that when he fucks her for so long without him releasing, she will continue to feel his cock inside of her forever. It will be as if he has somehow managed to clamp her open with his shape instead of leaving her with what his shape has lost inside of her. In this way, she will feel him stay with her, as opposed to her having to stay with the absence of what he was within her before he pulled out, before he left.

As she envisions her perfect lover, she actively pictures Ujjayi breath entering the lingam and keeping it incessantly erect: past the limits of penis and past the limits of spurt. This gives her relief of her most primary fear: in the context of its offer to her, a male orgasm might in fact be a popped balloon.

Pica

At first his parents thought it was just an oral fixation. I mean, kids are known for putting things in their mouths. They did not worry much: just took the grocery lists and love notes and put them onto high shelves, kept the clay pots too high for him to reach.

Over time it became more clear. Their son preferred clay and paper over food. Throughout his toddler years he would cry and reach from where he sat on the floor, strain up toward the high-placed items. He refused to just settle for gnawing on his hands or being satisfied with the banana baby food.

Years later, when the doctor told them that their son had an eating disorder that more often appeared in women and children than it did in men, they chose to view their son as a rarity. "Medical books oust the voices of angels," one said to the other late at night as they nodded and marveled, strategized together over wine. "As long as we find ways to help his diet stay balanced, what's wrong with him eating what he wants? We want him to feel healthy and confident; knowing his inclinations in a wholesome way can lead him through his life."

They were interested in schooling their son in independence. Once they made their supportive intent clear to him, he began to share with them how it felt when he ate the tarot cards. "I like them much better cut than I do folded. When they are folded, they hurt going down. I am trying to get at the *down* that is already within; that is the point, not the going-down."

They were seeing his details, the way his desires and feelings affected his body. It made them feel close to him to know him by his preferences. He began to show them more: gorgeous snippets, flashes of color, and words thin enough to go down without too much of a fight, but present enough to make their sweet son look like a God swallowing pigment: hue and pixel.

Perform bibliomancies of the body. Breathe and close the eyes as you put the fingers down onto a card. The place you put your fingers down on the card matters as much as which card it is: being led to where the cuts need to be made.

MALLEABLE ALLELES?

When she slept, it was as if her body was an orb of malleable alleles through which a peaceful God maintained the pieces of its peace by grinding into it, rubbing. Dough depends on perpetual knead.

When she woke from her dreams, she often called out to the fat air, whetting the space just before her lips. Contouring shapes can refine each other: from the soft of a mouth to the hard of a shout going into air, clear and sharp air driving the shout into a representative shape.

She felt comfortable calling out to air before she called her healer on the phone to schedule that day's treatment. Something about that order let her get some of what she perceived to be the toxins in her body (the toxins that drowned her in her dreams) out of her body before he even got to her house. She liked the feeling of having done her part, too.

As was usual for their sessions, with arms extended, she held the hawk wing with both hands out in front of her, trying to keep some semblance of poise about her while he draped her with the many yards of linens. She did not mind the covering part. She knew it was not about shaming or covering her up, but was an interim-cushion for the shape and heat of the weight that would come next.

He spent hours pushing the hot iron into the parts of her body where she had internal cysts. He was a strong man and, for her, he pushed with all of his might. They had decided together that he just might be able to iron them from where, without impact, the cysts would stay and strain her. They believed that he could force the cysts into evenness: something that her body could integrate. They decided together to have him iron her out.

She was so very skinny. The ironing left reddened streaks over her almost-bare ribs. Were these two obsessing together, an over-accentuated Adam and Eve? As was usual, red marks mysteriously spread over parts of the skin which were not even touched by the iron.

He has to keep his eye on the prize (the mid-section of her body, where the majority of the cysts are) or he can get distracted by her gaunt stature, and in that distraction, become intimidated. The sternness by which she grips the wing makes him fear she might crush it while he is trying to crush these cysts into something within her body that she can live with.

Is she in pain? She is not complaining, but he thinks he can see her feelings, there beneath her skin.

I is Iconic

When she returned from the war with such a drastic injury, they talked about her while she was right there. In other words, they talked as if she were not there at all. It disturbed them, the way she stared out the window incessantly, as if the Whidbey Island rain suddenly had something for her (when she had never even liked the rain before), as if that rain were somehow her new family. They never talked about that part: the disturbance, what she was to them now. It was her discovery that she was unable to bear children that had ushered her into that damn war in the first place, and now, back home, this grown woman depended on them like a child: at least that's how they saw it.

They all wanted their sister, daughter, wife back. They wanted her to continue to be able to be for them what she always had been before she enlisted.

To see the way that she sits, almost lifeless in her wheelchair now, causes them to have to leave the room with grief.

None of them agreed with her, initially, when she shared her decision to "Serve!" They thought the "Go Army" commercials were infantile, and the idea of their loved one responding with such urgency surprised and troubled them.

Her husband had always seen her legs as any husband would: sexy, objects for him. However, in the moment that she knew she had to go, she understood her own legs as very strong: strong enough to carry her across the globe, strong enough for her to be able to drag a fellow soldier out of enemy fire just prior to her getting hit in the face by a bullet.

OTHER EYES TO REPLACE OTHERING

It is of value to compose alternate histories. Alternate histories of a me through deviating cartographies means hope. Other (others') eyes enable me via surrogacy and intercession. It is possible to demand more than one-layer days, and to feel the colliding and chordate results of such demands. The results are in our overlap. I become more human when I can borrow your days for the sake of finding myself in mine.

Xe is frantic. With no idea where xe left xir journal, the fact that it had been left meant xe had made it vulnerable to being lost. Someone xe was possibly afraid of could be reading very private thoughts right now. That idea was terrifying. Xe pictured being found out, forced out of xir stealth, like when Susanna's journals were found and Lisa read them aloud to humiliate her, there in the basement corridors at the bottom of the ward in *Girl, Interrupted*.

It is useful for me to root in and extract meaning from other people's memories. I find that the more detailed the lists and images I treat in confidence, the closer to something I am getting. I am not sure what that something is, though. My memories are not mine. Like images, they own more of me than I have ever owned of them.

Ever since she found the mud-wrought notebook, she has been able to paint only one thing. Her boyfriend likes that, even though he liked her many paintings before. He tells her that within her paintings now, he always sees a daub-figure in consciousness-replication. This is a camber that does not close. It is not the same as how he thinks of karma: subjection to looping a tight circle until one can finally break out of it. The daub-figure now is not restrictive, but is recitative.

In the painting, an interior leverage is trying to spit itself into visceral appearance through both the pineal gland (pushing its way through the third eye from within the brain) and the

91

perineum chakra at the same time. Two extravagant places on the body that she is painting: kink by pixel.

After finding it covered in mud, after seeing colored paint marks which assured xem that the lost journal was in fact read while gone, xe has been writing many less words than ever before. Instead, drawings seem to be taking place by xir hand, regardless of xem.

If xe tries to control the arches of the aesthetic inscriptions too much, xe feels xir hand suddenly weigh too much. Xir pencil slips right off the page.

BIG SHOTS

For them, the shift began with what else they were willing to commit their mouths to.

Having long collaboratively engorged on the exudations: sweat and cum, those swells of mist on one another's genitals, they started to meet, nude, secretly, in the areas where the waterfall's spray met the water below it.

They figured it made more sense to enter moving water than it did for them to work in, say, a lake. There was the desire to keep the guttural pounding of sex near to them during this priming. Before finding one another, they were lonely individuals. They wanted their practice to relieve that and they both enjoyed how waterfalls have unconditionally liquid faces; they are presence while they are place. "Liquid faces last the longest; they surpass façade."

Face-up fodder is a form of bow. They are practitioners of their own vision and they agree that visions are body parts. Visions, much like human limbs, are upstanding instruments; they are for miraculous uses.

As they sync with each other by making their breath loud enough for the other to hear over the sounds that the waterfall is making, the trance starts to take them. Breathing into the waterfall, the two of them affect its flow. They like to be taken over, flooded in the place where water folds.

If they were to give themselves completely over to the pounding, then that would defeat their purpose; it would either push them out into the calmer surrounding water, or into the underside of the waterfall, where mold grows. While both of those areas are beautiful, these two are trying to stay together in a particular place: under the crystalline glow of the blow. Supporting each other in the eros of this beating.

As with any practice, there are always the fallibilities. Sometimes one of them is tired, misses the firm step and goes plummeting over to one side or the other: into the weight of the commanding wet. It is hard work to stand your ground to one of nature's marvels. They laugh, help each other up, even exchange kisses.

The fish look up at them with baggy eyes below the surface of the water. Are the fish weeping? Are the surrounding birds' songs getting heavy with more meaning? When these two manage to stay together, planted beneath the waterfall by the strong, circulatory poise of their posture, they feel one another drift into the other's vision. One of them holds an enormous string bass, playing it upright. The other is somehow elevated, as if floating on water, and playing a cello like a violin: big wood under a neck too small for it to easily fit. This is how to expand: employment of reach in regard to the untouchable. Discerning things about joy through the strength and stamina of another.

They were not disturbed by the extensiveness and drama of the shape from their current vow to their future vow. It was all view to them: plain and perfect.

They planned eventually, after many years of practice, to die together, face-up and eyes open, string music swelling their ears, under Niagara Falls.

THE *INS* AND *OUTS*: LIKE WICKER

After being shocked awake by it, there were times when what she
had come to privately refer to as her apocalyptic sense irked her,
felt traumatizing, made her feel that there were no others like her.
This type dies alone. "Okay, okay," she would shout into tarrying
images, images wherein the world would come to a flaming end
through her mother murdering her in front of a mezzanine full
of her own friends or the desert selfishly swallowing up all of the
planet's seas and their contents.

During such times, she felt preoccupied by sinister admixtures
and impending states; she feared being raped by collages: where
the sharp ends of images meet. Should she seal her eyes in an
effort to keep illusions out? Or should she tape her eyes open even
if the whipping sands of the desert were going to get inside of her
gaze? Should she turn the shower so hot that she has to literally
scream in order to stay in it? Or should she pack moist dirt over
the entire surface area of her skin and then go out and take public
transportation: her dirt dropping all over the city busses? How is
one with her predicament to best handle these: the apocalyptic
information itself, and the effects that information has on her in
form?

She would try many different things in an effort to soften
her flinch. She needed softening from so much flint. She was
on edge; she was an edge ever on the verge of burning. She
was entirely fight or flight and seemingly so without any other
option. Would she someday discover herself as a degenerate-yet-
procreant mission, incapable of continuing to live by desiderate
forms of tell, without these eerie circulations? Would she find
that these dizzying motions are an indelible aspect of her gift?

Spin the fluxes; put forth effort until the loom gets clogged,
then unclog it and continue in pursuit. Apocalyptic sense:

an ongoing awareness of a thing that is larger than life and simultaneously fixated on ends. Her apocalyptic sense: to say "I identify" is not necessarily an "I am" statement. She reaches to a motile North. Throat-frills develop in her story the more she learns to extrude beyond simple forms of negotiation. This world was never only for sitting on. If you're going to sit, relate to it: notice and be in awe of the wicker as it holds you up.

If you go further there is always more: voluptuous bindery, healing within blind wind.

IN THE THROES OF GMOS PART 2

After helping each other down the steep and slippery path, they sat by the stream. The ground sucked them in a bit (due to a certain constancy of weather). It ate their weight. They loved living in Oregon. They were currently homeless, and due to that fact, there was never a time when they did not feel the moisture of the geography they were in inundating them, soaking their clothes. They had done a lot together in order to get there. They were going to enjoy it no matter what. They were going to be grateful, even high, as their clothes molded while they were still wearing them.

They often recounted the memories, the work required in order for them to have arrived: leaving their past lovers, hitchhiking across entire states, sleeping by the side of the road in fear as insects crawled all over them, hearing the clear-cutting going on behind them and having to choose not moving toward it and throwing themselves in front of the saws that were being used to cut down the very trees that had called them there. They believed in listening to the invisible whispers, the compulsion of trees, no matter at what point in their morphology: from moist bark still attached to the tree, to moist wood fallen off the tree and into their hands, to writing on the intentionally dried bark as a form of paper.

Where they sat together, it smelled of piss and petrichor simultaneously: sort of amazing and also quite revolting. One of them asked the other, "Do you think that in our life we will see the end of things that grow? Will we be alive when the last flowers die?"

The other shifted position, lying with head in lap. The hair began to be stroked. The response was a reluctant one: "I don't think that we will see in our lifetime the end of things that grow.

97

I do, however, think it is possible that in the areas that put the most pressure on growth from the Earth, the flowers might just give up on us. If that happens, we will have to learn to relate to what we currently call weeds as forms of beauty and life, as something floral by which our breath can be taken away."

Imagining slightly decayed *Taraxacum officinale* growing in juicy groups; one nudges more deeply into the leg crease of the other. "The way that weeds have been typecast might have to change, too. Someday our preferences in regard to what we do or do not perceive as purely from source, might have to expand to include modifications. Maybe that will be how chromosomes become more tantric in the future: through practices that force them to change because we are changing."

What will result because we have changed important things that once were?

EPICENE

He cuts his hair short to match hers.

It matters to them both that she had short hair long before he did. He had been growing his out for her for many years until one afternoon when she told him she wished to feel the demeanor of his consciousness in a different way now.

To approach sensuality as a form, they actively imagine each other's genders and genitals; they induce variant expressions in one another. It is not so much what they inherit in regard to their own, but what they imagine of each other's: puberal wrangle in an ongoing queue, genders and genitals in eidolon, getting them off.

Harboring or harping on aphotic ardor, they are currently on their hands and knees on their apartment floor. They have been cleansing Bible pages together. First they tear and then submerge the papers until the ink gives out, turns to liquid again and fuses with the surrounding water. After the pages have been assuaged, washed clean of typical Biblical text, these two perfume them before perfuming each other.

Our bodies are our rites of passage: ways for us to face the sun. Both imagined body and plunged page are hope that helps us hoard each of our favorite versions of the wholesome costume.

HARD HELP

To them, chosen embodiment is an essential agenda, applicable in every era because of its capacity to replace essentialist forms of exclusivity in regard to how the body has been socialized to perform limits: to perform itself as a limit. They perceive the body as praxis: a way to breathe their own blood. They know themselves as the materiality of a portal's potential.

They wrap each other in animal pelts. The density and display of them stuns: faces smashing against each other's, hands pushing hard against hands. An onlooker might see their interactive engorgement as them hurting each other. They assure you: no hurting involved here. This is force with no flail. Their pelts are still bloody, pulled astonishingly taut around their forms. There is a sense of smothering by the other in their one another, as enablement.

Shamans of merge submerge burning candles. They are side by side and able to keep fire alive while the flames go below water. Feat is their fate. By using extraordinary qualities of authenticity and identity they assist each other in the many forms of travel.

One fashions a robe of leaves for the other, puts menstrual blood on the leaves and then spits in the milk. The drum, there, looks like a slab of meat: a lodestar lodged in the mud. Theirs is an evolutionary trial that is nomadic.

Those who live devotion are in constant need of devotion.

To Silence Pestilence

Even as insects shakily make their way up through all of the city's manholes, even as they thrum their way through the drains of your shower and kitchen sink and into your home to crawl over your diary, their low buzz with subliminal carnage inside of it is truncated: a noise-tendency pushing time and bodies toward no noise at all. Pestilence prospers in threats of impending silence.

To silence pestilence, please make all of the genuine noise that you can.

As one wanders out beyond the rim of neighborhood homes, one enters the nature preserve: a site of urban unruliness, liberation from the personas and panoramas of suburbia. One unloads every mahogany wooden frame (emptied of its picture) from one's son's backpack: a pack which one borrowed just for this endeavor. The unloaded frames are laid flat and pressed into the moist ground. Their placement is causing them to smash insects below ground as the ground gulps. At least half of the frames disappear below it.

One steps back a few yards: hand-on-chin observation and then shouts. One steps back a few yards more: hands-over-eyes and then shouts. When one is entirely screamed out, one collects every frame, returns each one to the pack without wiping the excess mud off of it. One ponders burning familial frames in synthetic forests. One wishes for more noir sound: mutters and rambles as one ambulates the bramble. One puts the pack back on and goes back, all the while in fear of a sudden, flesh-eating flash of locusts. One finds it within themselves to fiercely hum into the night's graphite: fear or no fear.

Pull the black linen off the old, dusty mirror. It is cracked. In the cracks, shapes are suggested. Work to make the mirror more rosy. A rosy mirror works images through it as a way of making itself come true. Each of the images in which it invests (by reflecting) is also a sound-making initiative. Sound is not a ruse; it is utterance as skilled movement of energy.

Voice is a substitute for pernicious, for sin.

ABIOGENESIS, AGAIN

She wished for herself that she would constantly compel catalysis.

She suffered whenever what she experienced of herself was not somatic buffet. In the years of her life, she had come to know herself as a way that something can always come from nothing. For this reason, in the few instants when she couldn't perpetuate, couldn't put out that something from nothing, she dreaded planetary loss of abiogenesis (in her own identity and body).

She recalled being six years old: remembered herself then, and did so without reminiscing. Her father's demeaning voice was a rush and a rupture. It made her feel like a bony vagabond, a moment's loss of itself, on repeat, continuing to reach for what else it might be. A six-year-old ravenously licking the algae and mold-soaked surfaces of the family spa was perhaps reason for some form of parental intervention, but not the way her father did it.

He refused to look at her inclination toward green gore. She did nothing to deserve the way that her father's grave and her own were in his stares as he belittled her. It does not have to be the case that you are free only until someone else tries to inhabit the place in which you are experiencing freedom. Inhibiting each other's inhabitation is not the only shape or shade of interaction.

When her father left, still mumbling his angry words with his back turned to her, she took off her shirt: did so because light had dipped its posture and dusk had arisen. She wanted it to swallow her slowly so she could dream of the pretty, effeminate men piercing her nipples, her lower lip and the webbed place between her first fingers and her thumbs. The pretty men were a way she could experience coarse caress. She knew she couldn't tell Dad about what happened with them at dusk. He would not believe her, and if she could prove it to him, even if she called them fairies, he would belittle her until (to him) she appeared smaller than he.

She felt her removal of her shirt as something she could hear: made her want to caress areas of herself until they rhymed to her. Her slow-moving hands across her own flat chest led her through the years until many years later, she got very robust, verdant vines tattooed over the varicose veins that had begun to appear on her body due to age.

MANTIC NAPE

Anthropophagous protagonists don't agonize, nor do they pathologize: they organize the particulars of their most-needed meal. Embodiments of masculinity are sought through long-practiced forms of magnetism. Grumbling guts produce fragrant and songly grease: ways to make a him desperate, ways to pull a him in. Astound by sound. There is a fragrance that only comes from him and the sirens permeate that as elemental, in a permanent way.

A siren's is a prevailing byway.

The blood is big-boned. It would have to be in order for it to call so many errant forms to emancipation via it. As self-feminizing ephemera, sirens are information addicted to calling other halves to them. What a relief to no longer be subjected to exorcisms, to the taking of information out of the body. Ecstasies are far more profound: information being pushed in.

Penetration of the sea takes place from within the blood of a femme fatale. Plush sonar skims along the protuberant rocks before his boat is turned to mush on their crannies, before his head knocks there, and he is knocked out. Will she find a way to knock him up, here on the ridge? What can she say? Catharsis attracts contrary healings.

Breasts with bird-sounds pouring from them emit from within the mantic, feathery cape. As they are ravenously taken, the cries of the lost *masculines* aren't malicious: they align. Siren cries are all-knowing. They require that you do things in order that you find what's on the other side of a seduction.

The other side of a seduction is never a solution.

Will-Force and a Wish

At the moment that she and her parents get to the top of the slope, she drops her mother's hand, snakes her way through the legs of tourists snapping photographs of trees and mountain details, and is finally at the edge of the cliff. Mother and father both have an eye on her; one eye plus one eye equals two eyes. Even if four eyes might be a better resource for a feral child making their way to the farthest-out (the most crumbling part of a ledge), two eyes is certainly better than one.

Father moves alongside child. It matters less if child sees him there; it's more important that he's close enough to her to intervene if she goes too far. On tiptoes with fingers outstretched, she is leaning far beyond the bar rail. Whitecaps of rivers mixed with air so far below are stimulation, are remembering and longing. Little body is a lid for a much larger living.

She thinks about the pine trees, how they look like a nest, seem as though they could catch her if her wings ever gave out on her. In the case of a healthy pine tree, where chlorophyll pumps and keeps leaves plump, is the tree ever anxious? Excited? She thinks about her parents: they kiss, they fight. Is flow in nature a constant, elegant elopement and envelopment? She leans further over the edge, trying to see.

With mother's two eyes, she tells father to go to child. Father decides to put hand inside of child's waistband so child can go far enough to see, but also not go so far that she falls. Father and child are both beyond the bar rail now. Child's little hands are dangling from her armpits down over the edge. Her eyes are pouring from their sockets, liquid-like, into the liquid and smearing forms below.

The wish: to be a child in a moving shell, swaddled in scapes, swaddled in scale.

DEBATING DECLENSIONS

They were in the town's amphitheater, debating declensions, when Mount Vesuvius blew.

As a community that often worked with apotropaion through representations of the genitals, their objects, hand-holds, décor and even their vegetables were inclined to ward off bad luck. Sultry shapes: cock-carrots, clit-peppers, hole-implications, anus-angles.

Flesh-prisms induce the exchange of fluids: many forms mix. His legs are above his lover's head as his lover pummels into him. Her legs wrap around him as he tells her that he needs her power of surrounding. Knees are being bruised while her butch lover, who prefers for her to grunt toward them in place of using a pronoun, nuzzles into cunt folds. They find work with anatomically correct symbols of their genitals far more useful and applicable than work with animal totems. This is what the back nook of the amphitheater is for: pearls being pushed into orifices then pulled out more porous, darkened in degrees by let.

The body is forefront because the body is both place and path.

Whether squatting or outstretched, entangled simply by proximity or by their own grip, the volcanic episode incites entelechy for them. Here are the frescoes that can only be found after the fact. Bodies covered in ash are a way to steer future generations back into events so that new insights regarding unencumbered eros can address apocalyptic abrasions.

The skeletons seem to be saying it to each other. The desire to fuck the human has put ash between them: is anachronistic lust.

GRASS

Allowing the body to lead is nature changing nature. He feels as if with every change he is literally flirting with weather as it relates to geography, courting Earth-in-variance.

His lisp is intentional; he gets men's attention that way and *man*, is he crazy about men. Sound and love in combination are the version of the alchemical wedding that he senses as most resonant for him. Sound and love are identity: his lover's growl, his squeal, such delight.

He likes bears the best. Their arms are a guaranteed swaddle that he could not wiggle his way out of if he tried. He likes it when his lover calls him "pretty girl." He is the pretty to a bear's girth; he is how a bear can wear a headdress of dandelions. He is a particular kind of he: pronoun for a process of she being integrated. As he strokes his beard while speaking, his lover's grip tightens around him with even more intensity. He needs to be crushed by a bear, made even more slender, able to fit into, then through, cracks. He is a pretty, skinny ringing, and his bear-daddy is giving him garish rings.

He is trying to tell his sweetheart not to be jealous of the way that he treats the weather: those endearing winks, tongue pressed in rimming-fashion against the misted windows, hands in the gutter in a penetrating manner and hair drenched in the first rain of the season. All of these are processes by which bottomless caress ensues. His lover is not jealous. He is and has always been a big boy.

When he seduces nature, he is breaking the sound barrier: making his way through the reflex-gallery and gathering details along the way. The more he runs his hands through the details like he runs his hands through his own long hair, the more he gets confirmation. Details are gifts from grace and they affirm our worth.

The man with whom he still lives (even though he never thought he would want to be tied down to only one bear) hauls around reams of grass in a large truck for his day job. When he arrives at the places where he is to drop them off, he literally unrolls the grass onto what was barren ground below it. The size of his bear-body and the size of his truck, both engaging this rolling motion, are arousing: turn him on at the level of his atoms.

He sees his bear as Adam, an indelible levee, a large structure on which to lean as he weeps at the beauty and bounty of this world. He weeps long and hard sometimes, into the falling rain, into the graininess of his bear's chest hair.

Memoir

Whether or not you know it, your relationship to words has always been an erotic one. The jar that hung from the ceiling of your truck, tied on both ends with purplish cording, inspired language. In it, you kept the bodies of dead moths that you found along the road: sank each one into the red wine within the jar that would swing while you drove along the winding mountains.

In the way that you are writing it, you are allowing trauma to both be addressed and remain open-ended. You approach the mystical sentence as a lyrical form capable of taking the tongue and other organs out of the body, one piece at a time. You do this for still-unforeseen forms of examination; your dreams are organs to you too.

Last night you dreamt of the place where Rumi still walks a labyrinthine implication of the body he once lived in. Rolls of Buddhist prayer flags were wrapped around the warped tree trunks of trees of which it is not possible to discern origin. As urged to, you went into the aphrodisiac shop in search of a poultice, a resource, a metaphysical reservoir from which to draw energy for your next encounter.

When in the shop, you were able to taste everything: vegetables and slabs of wood with carvings in them, inferences to carry your intuition into forefront. You got splinters in your organs. You wondered, when met with the information expressed by these carved inlets, if having sex with someone whom you were about to meet would help you find your way home.

GALLOPING THROUGH GALLANT

Even though she regularly defends herself against others' misinterpretations of it, maybe there is a name for this. Maybe it is in the DSM-5. Who cares? What matters to her is the tantric confidence that comes as a result of such profound intimacy.

She sees Lancelot everywhere. Lancelot is anything that pops out or is dramatic and in contrast to mist or fog: a field of open-winged shields, a place where wincing simply doesn't take place because there is no cause for it, no vicious predecessor. Her cavalier is a cusp and guarantees her indelible protection from predators.

She is drawn to the ideal knight: long hair and a high-held chest, unconditional exertion on behalf of women. Such gallant gallop through a galore of her is a singing. She is drawn to the sonorous presence of the courteous gem. The ideal knight rides through variations of night. Mist is a variation of night that, while it occurs at midnight, also marvelously occurs during the day.

She leaves the city as often as she can: the climactic moment being when she drives by the large gray-and-white bull, drawing it nearer to her. Sometimes she even stops her vehicle on the side of the road, and gets out, leaning over the fence with her hand and reaching toward it. Having recently come out as a lesbian, she hesitates before referring to a burly bull as, unquestionably, him. Though tough, and vital, like some of the butches who are currently opening her doors for her, this bull might be a her.

She knows she feels connected to this. She is not positive, however, if protection from predators is enough for her. As she spends more time with the bull, she realizes she might be the one who longs to protect. Puddles gather around her, are generators for her tongue-tied song. She thinks of *bull-her* dicks tucked below the belt. She considers erections shooting past the foreskin over the third eye as the third eye downpours, covers a scene.

Her own chest is lifting. The reflection in the puddle catches her attention and her eye simultaneously: explodes and implodes as it tangles with what she suddenly sees.

GORE SCORE

In music, there is a time signature but there is no time. What distinguishes a time signature from time is rhythm. Traditional time is a line; is incapable of engorgement. Music perpetuates feeling, engorges on what it distributes. By means of the rhythm that holds and drives music, time is released, time passes by, and time dies. Music is full of emotional significations: limps and upliftments, syzygy. While music is rich with timing, its power is in how it allows us to exceed time.

I still keep the small charm of an organ in the locket which hangs over my heart. I have not been able to help but keep it close to me since I first conceived of Saint Cecelia as progenitor. She set up her home as a church. She wanted to stay close to her God by tone and they killed her for it.

When the executioner tried to belittle her by beheading (knowing that the Roman officials had already attempted to kill her by locking her in a burning room) and was unsuccessful for the third time, I am sure that the drama of his footsteps (as he fled) could be heard as empowering rhythm by the villagers. What a model for resounding and reverberation! She sang and praised her rendering, her relationship with divinity as she lay dying, her throat cut but her head still very much with her.

I interminably prolong the ritual moment: do all that I can to never have to leave sacred space. My house is set up as a shrine too. I wonder what that makes them want to do to me. I can't help it: when I was a child, there was always music. There was the music I was playing and the music that was being played around me. Music is the marvelous stare into an aphotic state. Music is performance of stunning pirouettes in cream. I am a biophiliac of tones and timing, and while I continually leave time behind, I sing my chakras rhythmically: ally to a ceaseless peal.

WHEN INHIBITED, INHABIT TEMPERAMENT

The first night of the flood the lovers walked out in the rain together, sought puddles before puddles became screaming torrents. Reaching four hands in at the place where the flood waters were getting most raucous, they were soaked researchers looking for what to pull out in response to all that they had put into this. Pluviophiles hunger for awash: wash themselves in reveling instead of societally-modeled unraveling or rage.

"We believe that this kind of power can do it all for us:" nature as consort.

They have no children, so they are not the least bit intimidated when the images and photo streams of flooded schools begin to surface: paper, bins, classroom supplies all moving along the rigor of the water, being deposited into the forceful gushing of the river.

As they wade through the water, they are writing mental love letters to Pan: doing so from the perspective of Pan's offspring. The meadow is drenched. This is how what was becomes what is. The crops will grow with ferocity next year. A meadow full of water is a full bowl, a new lake where the dragonflies will come to mate, drawn by subvocal drives.

They both feel, that in a wet meant to sate, the wisest thing to hold onto is their visions. They kiss and whisper as they consider how Pan can keep operating when so far underwater: contorting the schist on which humans are trying to stand.

HAMMOCK-SHAPED HILLS

Hunger expresses itself as a seven-year itch.

A priestess meanders the edge. There is more to explore along the edge than the term edge presages. What just last week was a stream has become a river gulping at gulfs. The torn-down trees are simultaneously waddling in the deluge and hovering above it as they float. She is pursuing a juncture that contours the direction in which she is currently leaving marks: footprints.

She is hoping for a revelation. She needs to collage all of this energy.

Long having practiced collage as a form of love she believes in the moment when matter gives way to matter expressing itself differently. What is a priestess's role in a natural disaster? In a bloated rivulet? Is that role predetermined or self-invented?

Her stance is elegant anarchy. She is exaggerating her monstrous parts so that the herding froth does not exceed her: hands pushing already-large breasts together, she is turning her body into an applicable area. She is also moaning. This desert has been pounded. Desert being blessed by pounding is not only Biblical; it is also land-bliss.

A priestess travels to the river to add herself to its swells. She postures as if she is about to enter. In an effort at crossing to the river's middle, the midlines in her mind are flashing, exchanging sides. It is when two feet are in the surge that she decides to turn around for one last glimpse before going all the way. She twists her body backward to stare into vital collage; it calms her.

What she sees brings her from the burgeon and bellow back onto land: deposits of both whole and cracked eggs by the hundreds on the grassy knolls.

She 2

I am a martyr for a cosmic cause that's only barely coming into clarity. Dying both before and after cause is ever being fleshed out into clauses. Dying means waiting on more meaning. Dying is another version of holding more still than usual.

I perch myself in the upturned and continue attempting to peel the skin off of my own hands without any touch: I'm not touching and neither is someone else. Political third eye. My heart and my hearing can both exist there, together, as hearth. What else could prove a certain kind of human body legendary? Don't shut or shunt a tender body. Particular human bodies are a quiet skill that never need be stopped.

This is not a dry avocation for reincarnation. I imply this explicitly. A post-apocalyptic Eve might or might not come back to life. I might or might not come back as something capable of being signified by another's signifiers. I depend on the garden now. In the garden there is no polarization, no wish for something else nor wrath due to Adam. I had to let Adam go. I admit to you that, though challenging, it felt good to do so.

There is no such thing as general gore; it is possible to grow by explicitness, without girding, without holding grudges. The unseen-but-impending gore is what gets me off now: subliminal limelight being courted into form, counted on.

There is honor to be made on behalf of the delicacies of the garden. They present as dense and ephemeral. I must honor. Flow is onward-honor.

What connotes *she*? If given light unconditionally, then a prism is a constant dialogue with itself.

MOONWALKING IN THE TEMPLE

Premeditate by mantra.

As much as a mantra can be space's needed décor, it can also act as a relief agent. Sometimes a song is in you from before you were born. Sometimes you were born as unevenness in form. You can't name it any other way. There are parts of me that are not from here, so "I'm starting with the man in the mirror": with what I've got of *then* now.

Do the walk that is most natural to your body: a walk that moves forward and backward at the same time. It is a walk that reminds you of a woman in the moon (instead of The Man in the Moon) and it floods any stage on which you perform. You hope to walk the labyrinth of yourself, humming and channeling, until you die. To render yourself the temple that you are, you work with reflection as a way to change fate. Mantra can be used to mediate, to smooth twitches in human storylines by the sounds that come from within you, possibly from before your form in time.

When he sat across from you during relentless rehearsal, with that studded belt in his hand, what was he trying to teach you? Or was it about using your song, your intuited relationship to steps as lyrical, to benefit him? The incessant vomiting that occurred at the mere sight of your father indicates your fear, pain, lack of safety in your own body due to him.

Maybe your song is the most safe body you ever thought you could have access to. Is that why it seems that it lovingly folds itself around you, turning the ground on which you tread into clouds? Are you a living embodiment of cloud nine?

As he whipped you and criticized you did your father know then and there that he was taking your adulthood from you? You would eventually have buttons on your favorite jacket: buttons which mirrored the trinkets which once hung off of your father's erect and abusive belt. You would, of course, have debilitating nightmares, struggle with body-hatred, chronic sleep issues, and feel isolated.

The swagger that was present as you walked your way through your own voice is notable. Your falsetto was a hero: a way and a place for tomboys to wriggle. The aggressiveness of your growl, that hiss through clenched teeth, reveal that you were courting unseen forms of rehabilitation.

You wanted to "make the world a better place," buying land in Santa Ynez, having your kid through artificial insemination with the help of a surrogate mother, so you would never become your father in relation to having had a child in the same way that your parents had you. You wanted more tenderness than that; you wanted tenderness for you and your child both.

Suave can revert struggle.

During the strip-search the police violated you. As they were looking for the dark spot among your pink, between your legs, some of the rhinestones on your glove outright died. Your own magical hand was dying before your very eyes, while these surrounding men watched on like voyeurs. You could not believe this was happening to you, to the world. In that instant you had flashbacks of your father; the sweet and sonorous self-made glisten by which you lived, continued to fall off at your feet. You were the only one who could see them, the dying rhinestones. But your friends believed you. They knew that they were really there.

Your anorexia worsened. The afterlife neared.

In the afterlife the temple is hormonal; it has mood swings that hold you in all of your own swings. Moods and fluctuations are a type of map, a way for the lucid walk to stay lubricated. Tears and sweat in gyration produce ample rhythm, flood the road made of foreskin.

The luminous skin that you chose for yourself has to do with the way that the full moon makes you feel. It does not have to do with a desire to be a white man. You never saw yourself as a white man, no matter how many surgeries, how much change.

Your rhinestone glove is soaked. As the full moon reflects, your gloved hand floats underwater, partway below the surface of the wetness and partway above the bottom of the sea.

LIFE AND DEATH

For Lark Fox

When the moment for a meal finally manifests, its metabolism ravenously ricochets, physically increasing the size of the python's heart in just a short three-day period. Enzyme-gush protects the heart from injury, and this occurs just after the python has engorged. The body is a green area constantly being affected by reddening.

When she and her lover were walking around that particular bend in autumn, after following miles of winding Colorado rivers, did they expect to come upon a bloated man floating face-down in the place where the river had pooled? Pooled places in the river are the parts of the river that are decaying; unlike other places in it, the river can't keep these pools crisp. Elementals are for insatiable witness of them: the compulsion to get involved. Codes are carnal ephemera.

The fact that there was not even a pause in her gait when she saw him there was surely indicative of something particular about the nature of her own pheromones and heart. She couldn't keep her body out of this moment. She hurled herself into the stagnant water. She had been trained to bring air into moments such as these: not trained by paramedics, trained by mystics. How far back did her lover stand while the mosquito-wrought, algae-rich water stained the white apron she had chosen to wear that morning? While she sort-of choked on the imprints of decay? Did she prefer that her lover recede in this moment, so that she and the drowned could protrude together, possibly collaborate some form of life-giving magic?

Can the face-down-drowned be brought back to life? Ask Ophelia. She pauses as she sees her. Says "Ophelia" to herself in her own mind as if calling for direction. She tilts her head up and into the flood of sun between each blow. Feeling the crunchy autumn air as drastic in relation to the sun's sleek, she glows. Giving a drowned, bloat-bodied man mouth-to-mouth on a cool morning is a fragment. Fragments aren't for misery but for mystics. Ultimately our enlightenment has to do with what it is that we did with the anxiety that we have had since before we were born.

Perhaps it was only after hours of private work, wherein he remained motionless to her breath, that she wished she were giving mouth-to-mouth to a drowned woman. That image would have been cohesive with her recent work with the Goddesses. She had fantasized many times about making out with a Goddess, even attempted divining ways to make that possible.

Her gestures could be seen as a trust that Earth will speak to her moments through fidelity: a dynamic allegiance.

Slide

For Elizabeth Robinson

After many days of a consecutive nightmare she was waiting in stillness in the single bed, forcing herself to stay awake until she really fell asleep. She thought that perhaps if she made herself fall, she might fall into something new: unexpected undulations with sudden swains in them.

She enjoyed dreaming of butches and land: lovers saving each other from quicksand. It was the erotic masculinity that kept calling her back to this place. Ever since she had moved out of the house that she and her husband had previously shared, she had seen more of herself in the tough world: the world where strong lovers paint mud on each other. Mud is awakened; it doesn't prefer one thing while subverting the other. Mud keeps love active and in doing so increases life.

You realize there is always so much that could have been done and you realize this as the rain of the storm is pounding, as the lips of the rivers are stretching beyond themselves.

When she could hear the water changing the color of her carpet, she chose to keep the light off. She thought to herself that if her small room in this basement was going to be washed away she could at least choose to keep the canvas of darkness in her eyes. After all, darkness was where she dreamed: agencies of lucubration as the lugubrious cadence forcibly aerating the scope.

The viciousness of an abrupt crash just outside made her jump up onto her bed. For a moment, her knees went soft, taking in the subtle bounce that can be felt on any bed, no matter how old it is. It is amazing how much you have access to in a simple moment of memory: being a child and using coos to communicate. She had a severe longing and it made her lurch. She had to call her loved ones, speak to them in clichés and easy phonemes, and had to do so right now. Even to simply say their names (those that she and her husband had chosen for them so long ago) in her children's presence would be enough.

The desire to make the phone calls forced her to turn on the light: mud sloshing all around in currents and pools at the base of the bed. There is no way to prepare yourself for the way that introduction of just one more sense during a natural disaster can literally alter the atmosphere of what of you might remain after that disaster has passed.

Macromancy

Divine clout is a marvel. I have been held in marvels throughout many lifetimes. I had no idea when born this time that I would be born by metal: an animate display of rust. What I learned: born by metal does not necessitate living for metal. Each building wall, truck-tire, broken window and piece of the road are tools.

On the day that it shifted, on the day of the difference, I went from seeing myself as something capable of mechanically making nature (but still very displaced from nature) to identifying as nature itself. Edenic identity presenting as corona-shaped: an unconditionally green crowning. Spewing anti-aporetics and herbs, nature is a prophetic form of machismo.

Self-naming is my right to a rite by which I might burgeon. In my favorite version, all of a world's concrete is exploding due to unforeseen forces of botanical gore. Is this an inversion of apocalypse? Accidental abodes spring up as if it were unavoidable for them to do so. People wear shirts that name it: tree bursts through concrete. How else but by excesses could land ever experience orgasm? For as long as I have felt myself as a disconnect from nature, I have also loved, lusted and longed for land. Regardless of what they try and tell you and how they may work to convince you otherwise, metal does long for and lend itself to land.

I try to avoid faux expansiveness at all costs. Divinatory work with realms would prefer my exertion as a gentle and honest version of a once-almost-entirely metal mechanism over a false inflatedness or illusory grandiosity. If I present myself as I am, then I can be magnetized toward who I might become while having bouquets of edible herbs wrapped around my eyes and mouth, around my neck: the relief of nature's noose. Fierce mustards, lemon balm and turmeric are all here with me in order to unleash, reverse the tamed and urban meme. This mission of Edenic mastery intrigues, completes. Plants are tractions, willforce in the intuition alerting the physical form toward alteration. Small sprouts are spreading through my hinges; they are a kind of oil to the Tin Man's creak.

Divine clout delivers: is for turning concrete cloth, into cloth. Regardless of what how it seems may connote, concrete cloth becoming cloth is not a return to or a circle. My becoming forest over time is not a salvation. It is a thorough evolution, an essential progress. What comes afterward? Green comes afterward.

Miracles are unexpected. What if we, with awe, began to treat them as something to expect?

Longing for living could result in this: a cyborg practicing and flourishing in a pleroma.

Unexpected Consort?

When they found her body on the mountain slope she was covered head to toe in bloodstained animal fur. This was not fur piled atop her. It was fur that had obviously been sewn into a fabric-form able to encase her.

As soon as the medical examiner had her in his autopsy room, and opened her legs, following procedure as usual to fill out the rape kit information, inside her he found something that shocked him. Finding a dead woman inside a fur-wrap in the woods might imply what he found, but it still fiercely rocked his perception.

Within her vaginal cavity: hundreds of small toothpick-like slivers bound together with a deteriorating string. What were these? Porous, yet smooth—bright bone-white.

When he got the results back from the lab he blanched. Did she put these into herself? So many penis bones from dead animals gathered together like a bouquet or bushel of dried herbs within her carnal canal.

Not as Simple as Before and After, but What Remaining Authenticities Continue to Come *After* After?

He passed after his surgery, but he still refused to be a man in the American-Man-as-procurement-and-fulfillment-of-the-American-Dream sense of the term. He was never, in all of his years, trying to be his father or any other Chief-of-Staff, Head-of-Stead.

He hated the idea of being on top of. His transition did not place him on top of the world. In fact, he was not a top at all. He liked much better the feeling of being an abyss's tip: a far edge of its emanation and expression. Yes, he had a dick, but he was also a resonance who would use his dick in that way: as a wand, treating his wife's body as she would have him treat it: as a scarred scape in need of scrupulous healing.

She kept telling him that this part of him was a blessing for her. She could only proceed by way of that shape on him. Endlessly snapping and unsnapping his lover's corset, day in and day out, he would always take his time with her, notice her as he pulls her apart and then puts her back together with his dick, of what she declares so desperately that she needs of him.

They wanted their life to be a form of meat, for it to feel like outstretched meat-curtains even though they were both long-practicing vegans. They considered themselves the other halves of things: half-moons, halves of watermelons. Veganism, for them, is political: restraint from an aspect as a form of giving life to life, as a way of filling things out. As they threaded their diet with food combinations and non-meat proportions that would keep them feeling full, he perceived them as incessantly sucking off the muse.

127

He read his wife's writing as ink being poured over vegan forms, ink pooling in the meat curtain, the cosmicity of folds. Bardos could be surpassed in this way, he thought: being the thing as opposed to consuming it.

He strokes her hair as the light in the room changes how her hair feels in his hands. They talk about how hair is slow-motion time, time as a rich expression of the agency of lovers: the only type of time in which they can believe and invest.

LUST

When I say I lust for land I do not mean that I long to own it or even to top it. For me, lust is draw toward convergence. I want to converge so deeply with it that I am in fact indistinguishable from it: a land-miracle, a green that spins more green. I suppose it is most appropriate to say that I lust after *land* as a way to invert losses of many types.

As lovers and makers of books, adoration and courtship by page is good. However, it is not good enough to simply stop at that. The memories of trees as timbre, in the blank pages that we hold in our rooms, will haunt us if we don't seek more of their source alongside them. We love pages; we are green's ally. Can a human be a surrogate for alteration of a tree's losses? Should we not throb with them, press our bodies into them until units of bark are embedded beneath our skin? We must enter the forest, advocate for green in places where there is no separation of us from it. Although page-based mirrors are enrichments, it is never enough to live solely to court the other sides and other lives of dead things (trees included). We will only die in the process.

All forms of life emerge from dark interims. Darkness is a known precursor to green. When live trees taught me this, there was a lot of bark pushed beneath the topmost layers of my skin. I moved from staying on Earth only by self-made bondages by pages herein to coming up from Earth in rooted ways. A human can be a literal root of the Earth, and a root is not time; a root is intimate relationship with.

This is what it is like, naturally in my body, when I am a living mother of many offspring-pages and have a mother in Earth with which to relate: a living mother who is not only blood lineage (which can also be a blood limit) but who is also unconditional lifeline. A suitable cosmic mother would have a fractal face: face that sucks on my very human face. My erection (which is located in my third eye) protrudes, ever reaching toward and through the bark of old-growth beasts. Embodiment of bark happens; my erection explodes, leaving me as a mammy fungal gown producing glowing jam on the perimeter.

An orgasm is a natural extreme. Weep into my eyes, mother, so I can see the sodden erections that trees keep beneath their bark. In the aspen forest I turn my face up to the sky. I let the rain fall into my eyes.

RAINING ATOP OF A SALTY WATERFALL: A MINI-MEMOIR MID-BOOK

After so long in practice and seek, I have found my mother and my husband, and they are both queer women.

Collaborations Corroborate

Collaborations are a type of land, a way to set something natural in motion. Collaborations can be land that lasts forever. Collaborations are an ethical approach to additivity. We hold hands as we pull subjects apart: reveal subtexts.

Distortion is pleasure, a way to heal. We do not distort in order to take things away from one another, but in order to augment. Supplemental psyche can induce relevant nakedness. What comes out of the extreme is conical.

She had become quite familiar with the alphabet of their strum as a constancy inside of her: muse, angel, and siren sounds resounding in the woods. Sometimes she felt sure she was being operated upon by this: a permanent part of the music.

However, it was when her lover told her that she heard it, too, that everything changed.

We track kinship by the muses that we share.

SIREN SOUNDS SMEAR THE SKIES OF A LAND-LOCKED STATE

It was in the way he lifted her: first very low, almost causing an inverted curtsy, and then up and up beyond all encrusted visage. He was not a man, and he was certainly not a woman. He was something else entirely. Because he was not hindered, because he was steady, she perceived him as a clean-cut-stronghold turning into tears and ice.

In her dreams, she had long been visited by a genteel Frankenstein. He propped her up so the weight of her entire body could rest on the curve of his skinless, large knee. He felt familiar to her. What did not feel familiar were the grandiose tankards in the background, the enormous chunks of concrete, and the alluvium deposits shaping and reshaping the shades, inundating the cues.

In order to not block them out, in order to identify with what was not familiar to her, she needed to perceive the unfamiliars' enormity as nature: floating in the froth of the sea and not disappearing below it. To do so required an absolute floatation device: a dream boat.

A dream boat is a bias toward bliss.

CHORDS: THE VERTICAL ASPECT OF MUSIC

Ions covet coverlet: the array continually arranging and rearranging itself from beneath the protective sheath. Ash is blown across the cool pigment of the floor. The room is curved. Windows, slightly ajar, are miracles; they let myopias in and out at the same time. When we share in the space in which we reside, we are finding ourselves in one another. If I could give you the bone that you need, then I would pull it from my own curved side, dusted in affective powder.

With awareness, he sings melodramatic harmony alongside the Buddhist lama's melodious drone. Together, he feels himself and the others as shared space, unconditionally christening the ashram: Buddha-shaped burgeons, big-bellied blessings.

Even though, at first, he got looks from other practitioners (after all, he was causing his breath to moan) he felt that they soon got used to him, how he sounded in practice. Om is an expanse capable of holding more than one lyrical quaver. Harmony: a natural inclination of his body toward being uninhibited by thoughts.

When he is involved in harmony he feels himself free of logic, dreaming the sound-key to unlock pi. Keys are right here with him when he is right here in a chord. Keys: plush and permeable wads taking presence far beyond wager.

PURLOIN LOIN

They had been monogamous partners for many years and they were still having a lot of really good sex. Their needs were mirrors: mirrors as places to harvest cracks in mirrors. "The crotch is a split in the legs for a reason." They appropriated each other's sexes as a pledge to the ability to offer each other range: a gurgling, heart-shaped henceforth, an effervescing ever-after.

In an unconditional romance with the edges of one another's bodies and identities, it worked for them to take from the well without asking. They preferred to have no safe-word. For them, a private pronoun could be a form of kink.

While taking from each other, in fact, made them both feel very safe, secure and satisfied, there were not always orgasms without more being sought. There is always more in there than there seems to be. Some underwater caves keep small pockets of air in them. In order for orgasms to take place between them the image of those pockets had to be penetrated, filled up with a force of liquid or petals or human fat. Water needs to douse in order to feel itself as fate. It was the image of caves in lucid weight that eventually made them cum.

Steep Spadix

They are all invested in the phenomena of pliancy in forms perceived as inarguably hard or phallic. Copious and arresting phytochemicals spew from the erection which protrudes from a crease in the floriated corpse.

While some botanists are busy comparing the lengths of their *Amorphophallus titanum* blooms, others are passionately crushing up the male flowers of their plants in hopes of eventually exposing the power of the flower's ability to pollinate itself. Both approaches require hands-on tactics: stroking down the character of the inebriating shaft, gripping soft-tipped paint brushes as the pollen is distributed along the receptive gradient of the pistil.

In the Victorian era girls were deliberately kept from seeing these flowers. There was drama about it. I imagine some of the girls had to be dragged from the flourishing sites with their whole bodies in the shape of an outstretched hand: a hand reaching toward what is compelling them because of its smell. Sometimes there is no need for sight. A voodoo lily communicates with a hysterical girl subliminally, by any number or type of somatic undergrowths. What do you smell in pheromones? Cheese? Death? Moth balls? Depth? Petrichor? Spice? Chocolate? Do smells make you moist? Pheromone distribution synthesizes a girl's future of subversive sex, long prior to her investing too much in the aesthetics or the technicalities of it.

Amorphophallus titanums prosper in disturbed grounds. Modern girls are already secondary forests: natural progresses neighboring what are often the disturbances between the men and women to whom their births can be credited. "Were my parents really that drunk when they conceived me? No wonder they can't stand each other. I never saw them love each other: not a day in my life. I have heard from them, more times than I would like to admit, that I was a mistake."

Aroma volatilizes in order to pull: carrion beetles swarm in from miles around for their chance at pollinating a meaty marvel. A girl presses her whole body against the steep spadix; she doesn't only use her hands. A girl becomes a woman who ponders decaying life-forms daily: the world's largest and most rank flower included. A woman who was once a girl (surrounded by men who were trying to keep her from sentient sex) ponders what her loved ones might someday be compelled to say at her funeral.

Possibly, finally, outright waft: sentences of unabashed sentiment.

EDGE

He noticed his books began to fall apart when his life fell apart: glue gathered as globe-shaped globs in the creases between pages before the pages fell completely out. He was flaccid: both dick and heart. His gaze was lethargic. His posture indicated how he felt about himself, his own well-being: torpor, unavoidable heap.

He placed the toes of his bare feet over the ledge as he began to throw the pages of his books into the sky. He perceived them as flying upward even as he watched them fall hundreds of feet below onto the city streets. His legs and hands were shaking. "It must be cold up here," he thought, not having really noticed it before. Flurries were slowly soaking the pages in his hands, the pages in the air. His eyelashes were getting caked too: the detaining details of a New York winter.

A few people had begun to gather below. He could not really see them from where he was, so many stories up in the sky and at such a physical distance from them. He was not exactly thinking of jumping. He hadn't really thought about that at all yet. He was busy with pages.

Regardless, the cops busted through the door with their commanding. "Great, just what I need: more reductive men." He said this under his breath. He was here and also beneath himself. Page by page he experienced a temporary high in the uplifting throw as he watched the page soar, and then felt the undertow, tide-like pull: gravity bringing pages to the ground.

As they set up the catch-net at the base of the building he experienced a momentary frustration. "I guess I have no choice in this." How did the cops hear about him? What neighbor called on him? He had come up here quietly. He had not been disturbing anyone.

They were making his edge a spectacle. "Oh, forget it. Never mind:" Bent over, breathing heavy. He dropped all of his pages from his hands. A piece of a snow-soaked page whipped backward and sliced into his eye.

He turned his back to what could have been his own grounding end. As he walked back toward the door he had entered in order to get up here, there were hands on him in an instant: cops-weight weighing him down. He would go back into his apartment after meeting with his therapist. He would keep writing the words "tough sure" as ointment onto new pages, then onto his white walls: intention coated with black pastels.

On the Eve of the Harvest Moon

There are ten figures standing by as abrupt erections in the field. The figures seem to be poring over pie tins full of milk. Their straw bodies in extended posture bring them nearer to cream. On the steps just outside the farmhouse door, cardamom colors act as contours to the colors of the dark sky. The full pie tins are drastic comparisons. Objects share with personage. As the sky continues to darken, objects and personages have the right to intentionally sleep.

The small bits of fur and feathers glued to the scarecrows make them appear as lucid dramas against the dried corn stalks in the field. Pumpkins are rolling around at the base of the scarecrows, filling in what could have been a gap due to scarecrows having no feet. Is a scarecrow, sleeping in an autumnal field a foreigner to it? Or is a scarecrow, by design, one of autumn's phantom limbs returning to it—a way for autumn to express itself?

Even though I can't hear them (I don't speak hay), I can feel the conversations that the scarecrows are having. Thunder claps, and more of their secrets and dreams ooze from their stalks, their interiors. Whispers are carried from field to field: carried forth by their catching in an unexpected socket and then rolling along the pygostyle of erratic flying fowl.

Rural Sinkhole

Was it the collapse of the roof of a hidden cave that caused that particular sinkhole? Or was it the gathering weight of additive materials on the surface? Was it the flow of liquids below the topsoil that weakened it? Or did the turning of water-flow into acids do it (based on their participation in botanic procedures)? The couple who had lived on their farm for many years had no idea that the sinkhole even existed until *the event.*

Urban sinkholes swallow cars in a fricative gulp. The rural sinkhole on this couple's farm was responsible for a blind stallion's fall even further from power: a once-authoritative beast being trapped below ground. Even though he was now blind due to age, they had decided not to put him down because they had spent years training him and he could still be ridden: just needed to be a bit more led than he used to.

They did not perceive their land as endangering him. In fact they had seen it protect him, engender him in the past. They had sensed their land as something that actually held him up in his power. They were very familiar with the hoof marks he made in the fields. They read his marks (more than the marks of the mares) as a way of tracing time. Were his hormones thrumming through his legs today in ways that would cause him to flap his mane and overarch his neck? Make a ruckus? Or was he exhausted, choosing to lie on his side and rest even under the threat of crushing his own internal organs? This couple concerned themselves with his story. They considered him a force of nature, even their friend.

Lately he had been getting along relatively well with the mares: tended to keep quiet and still at night, stand alongside them echo-locating by their breath more than being their aggressor. His boisterous galloping and gallantry seemed to be slowly subsiding. He was presenting more like a mare than he ever had. It was as if, over the years, alongside his blindness worsening, he had been made into equalizing or equanimity: a literal body on which it is possible to watch patriarchy wear itself out.

The veterinarian had said that the stallion could still see shadows. The couple on the farm thought that that was perhaps all he saw. One night, a blind stallion falls into a blind area on the land that once held him up. The night's mist deepens around the sinkhole. It is so tight down inside of the hole that he can't even pace. Stallions that no longer regularly run need to pace. Mares, with their blinders on, slowly gather at the edges of the hole: a circle of them leaning over what had previously topped them. Snorting, they go no further than the edge. They manage to not follow or fall.

Are they relieved to have him below them, finally? Do they perceive themselves as topping him now? In the rural sinkhole a blind stallion can't see the mares that are leaning over, and the mares, with their blinders on, can't see down into the contents of the hole.

Tracking lifelong damages in a moment can be a double blind, as nays and snorts deepen the wayward night.

KANGLING

Whenever xe dreams subliminal speeches regarding seminal sentience xe wakes up with a sore throat.

The first time xe saw the phallus-shaped crystals protruding from the moist dirt of the mound xe stopped mid-gait. It was hot outside, mid-summer and xir body was shivering from somewhere deep within it: buzz quaking up and out from between skinny, hairy legs. Ripened by ritual apparatus, a queer human body is a transitory cave making its way through modernity. What xe had just stumbled upon was the most perfect way possible to explain xir reality: queer cock.

Having searched for ways to explain for so many years, there had always been a gap between what xe felt xe knew while fucking and how to explain that knowing to others. Xe had both queer and not-queer friends and it felt important to be able to articulate the rising hub of xir desire to both groups.

Shamans soak their objects in magic, and by that practice, objects come alive. Xir kangling: an integral shamanic tool rising between the legs in order to assist in making one's way into and through the needed trance. Cock rises as animation of a very distinct, but blur-based body. Elastic dance turns the organs into amulets. Marinating in raw elegance manifests a cock that will never go limp from loss of essence. The Underworld is perking up, expressing itself as dark liquid gathering in a tar-like pool between realms. Xe bends down and fingers the wetness. Xe licks the colored liquid off tips.

Spirit Bear

Neither albino nor polar bear, the spirit bear is a black bear born with white fur. Never spoken of by locals over dinner, it is perceived to be a sacred form. Locals don't hunt sacred forms. They would prefer to sip on simple soup and imagine a black bear with white fur making its way through an old-growth forest's vertical piths.

As it safely inhabits pause, the mutated gene amplifies, ascends. Herein pause becomes plural. A single, mutated black bear is the swell of embodied halo in a forest. As it eats it envisions itself as excess to spectrum. It devours more than eighty salmon in one sitting.

XYR

Something about it still wasn't sticking. Sure, some people were responding to xir demand of accurate reference, but something about the pronoun was still a tiny bit off. Xe could feel it. Even though xe described it as rhyming with *fur*, xir also rhymed with *her*, and the sound of that pronoun brought the body back to the initializing site of the first trauma, the birth trauma.

Driven by what xe had been known to describe to xir friends as xir raw, chain-link heart, xe places xir hand over the cracks in the greenhouse. Xe fondled the sprigs shooting out of the dome through those cracks as if it were still spring, always spring, when in fact it was the protective dome, built specifically for them, that allowed the core of these plants to live, that covered them from the ways that winter harshness could damage them. "With the core protected, the shoots are free to burst through the cracks. I believe that a pronoun can be like that," xe mumbled. "As true on the atomic level, as encompassing in its procreant aggressions as it is a social compass."

There was no creation myth with which xe identified. Xe thought perhaps that fact and feeling were because xe was a creation myth: a loom riddled with many lures. Maybe a slight change being applied to an already dramatic change would in fact suffice. "Yes, *xyr*," xe mouthed.

Xyr: a studded swain, a cyborg cavalier. Xyr rhymes with seer.

METAPHYSICAL BUTTER

Sometimes, when driving along the back roads between towns, you spend so much time in your car that you forget that it is as much of a public space as it actually is. Don't get me wrong. It is good to feel safe in public spaces, and to feel as much is often a rare experience, but the buck tapping on the grasses to the side of you is watching you as you drive. When you are in traffic, look at the man to your right. He is listening to talk radio and picking his nose with no thought that you might in fact be watching him like television. You are hoping to pass some time seeing how deeply he will dig for gold before noticing that you are staring.

When the officer finally got the driver to stop, the officer exited their car with caution. The driver of this vehicle had been winding over the delineations between lanes and had been doing so for many miles. This was not just one instance of breaking the law; the officer knew that the driver had not just taken their eyes off of the road for a moment, in a one-time case. They were probably texting and driving, the officer thought, making a snort and slamming their door.

When the officer neared the bloody window the reach for their gun was immediate. At this point the officer thought that it would be best if the figure behind the window did not open the window just yet. What was going on here? The officer needed time to assess.

There was a forward, pointed knocking on the window itself, and then the muted sound of instructions going from outside of the car into it. The driver knew they had been caught, but did not understand what the big deal was. They moved to open the door: a gesture to which the officer responded by slamming it back shut on them.

Now, from the inside of the car, the muted voice of the driver

146

moved toward the officer: "What do you expect me to do? Just sit here? What are you waiting for?"

From officer to driver: "Roll down the window slowly, sir."

As the driver does so, a woman is revealed behind the window. With a quizzical look in her eye she lifts her hands up to show the officer the contents within them: menstrual clots. "Don't worry, officer. There was no murder here. I was just trying to gather. I don't like to waste." Menstrual blood can be used as a lubricant for masturbation. She thinks that the officer is obviously not thinking of that particularly wise use of clots in this moment.

The officer's face blanches. The driver's hands are full and as the officer stares, she pours the contents of her hands out onto her lap: a bloody puddle on top of her legs as addition to the bloody pool between them. She extends her stained hand in the officer's direction.

"So are you going to give me a ticket or what?"

A Totem You Can Wear

On the evening that the earrings began to fall from the sky into the sea, the female anglerfish was feeling especially unified with him. However, this was not always the case.

It is not easy sharing your body with a small but assuming male. His appointing of her as his homeland and his continued anointment of her lately had made her circulatory system softer to him, more available. He had linked into her so long ago, and now, together, their bodies make it physiologically possible that *a he is literally unable to let go of a her.* (Parasitic processes allow him to be her.) What are the ethics involved in sharing something like this: the dynamic miracle-body in abysmal lurk?

Earrings are falling down through the deep, catching flecks of light in the process. The angler couple thinks this might be what weather feels like to humans: something that stuns you as it passes you by.

They try to notice by staring at the event separately and find that she is too strong in comparison: an unintentional Goddess. If you can make it work, a self-made gender at the bottom of the sea is an enigma in which to share. What is shared can connote safe space. She is the totem that he can wear. Her size and vigor make him more notable. Notice how the spectacle of her aesthetic contrasts in relation to him. Look at how bland and at a loss he would seem without her nature adorning him: the jagged headdress of her curved teeth, the flashes through her translucent skin revealing red, thread-like nerves as ribbons teaming across a stage, the sandstone and burnt-sienna color of her exuberant skin as a cape to cover him, quaff him into wholeness.

Looking in the same direction is never enough for them: too much tug when you are toggled like this. Swimming alongside one another in order to mate (as is the case with salmon) is just not going to work. They have to find additive ways to ensnare each other and the fact that other anglers had done so over many hundreds of years prior to them (made species evolution possible for them) made them know that they could make more closeness even as they differed so dramatically from one another.

Single earrings fall, penetrate the surface of the sea: cut through froth before falling lower, leaving typical light behind. As they fall the singles brush up against other singles, knocking off paint flecks or small jewels to be absorbed into the abyss. Earrings falling through the sea hope to find their matches. When they become entangled by interlocking designs or by earring hooks getting caught in other earring hooks, they understand that a beloved match is not entanglement with the same earring but with a shameless and shapely, often unexpected, contour.

It is possible to protrude together and it is difference that brings on an equal profusion.

SOMETIMES THE LOVER JUST NEEDS

Sometimes a lover just needs a break. They work at a motorcycle shop or a boot-repair shop and their hands and minds are tired from so much traditional manual labor. Sure, Rumi coached society to "let the lovers be," but who besides them and their own lover regularly even read Rumi? Certainly not anyone who works alongside them in this shop. You can't really tell your boss or your buddies that you know that your body is for a different kind of manual labor—cosmically—than the kind that you spend your human life doing: at least, you can't if you hope to continue bringing in a paycheck.

In regard to the average Joe, more time is spent drooling over newscaster's presentations of whatever's currently being termed a "national disaster" than attention is being spent on the appearances of sudden *sodden* in odd urban settings: those uttering jewels and myopic portents that occur during natural dealings.

Mist has om and loam in it. When the mist begins blocking out the windows, the lover knows that the aspen leaves outside will look most like fire in the next few moments of their progression. There is urgency to the need to break away now. The puffy edges of the shells of thistles will be pouting, gently spewing their seeds out of the puckers in their forms. This is the pocket being sought. Now is the time.

A lover wanders through the aspens along the path: does so long beyond the strictures of their authorized hour-long lunch break. Paper-thin golds are being collected by hand and placed in the shirt pocket: little moments of metropolitan scald.

IN THE BEGINNING

Xe did not come from a nuclear family. Xe had never even set foot in a church, so it was not that xe believed in the Bible: no inner compulsion regarding the Bible at all. Xe just happened to be able to feel some precipices as compulsive vibration.

Lately xe had been preoccupied with words as the first elemental in which xe ever felt a sense of self, a genuine desire to be in the world *as* world and not as doomed to a fate of being something foreign to it. Words were the only nature that came before nature in the order of things regarding xyr form, so when the pastor quoted John 1:1, xe was awestruck, thinking the pastor to be speaking directly to xyr own thoughts.

A thought showing love to words, without it yet having been pronounced as words, is a dream anxiety: a landlocked beat. Without really trying to do so, xyr hand began to outstretch beyond the sieve-like sleeve of xyr cape to take the pastor's already-outstretched hand. Then the pastor led xyr body into the church as if in a subtle dance, as if xe were following. Was this following? Xe felt the movement in slow motion. In transition, xe noticed things. Leaves were moody: nooks catching greens, yellows, reds and purples.

"They are words within before they are ever thorax and then throat, before they are ever words pronounced," xe began to say to the pastor before he turned around and left: leaves caught in the undersides of his robe. There was more work to be done out in the cold, it seemed. Xe turned slowly toward the hearth and saw people kneeling. There was a glow in the space. Xe squinted. Was that meat falling from the effigies? Xe reached up and gripped the locket around xyr neck.

... "and the word *was* God" resounded through the shape of the church. In response to it xe felt a slurping buzz as if wasps and

vultures were inside xyr cape, very near to xyr own body.
A wintered Lancelot-lace-clot is vigil in vigor's field.

CAN FOREVER BE FORCED?

There had been quite a few yelling matches between them; they had even questioned calling each other best friends anymore. Where they used to sit together with their legs outstretched into the streets at midnight, talking and laughing beneath that old streetlight, she had now been sitting alone for many months.

Pictures are not mere mental projections. Presence of pixels is not indicative of, nor is it permission given for anyone to separate. Even though she had been sending her subliminal pictures of roadkill as a way of trying to accurately speak to her in a language of her own pain, she knew that there was something wrong with the gap that she was also allowing to take place. She just didn't know what to do about it in their situation. She and her old best friend had collapsed into a human trap. Their egos were obviously invested in keeping their own piece, and that fact made for little to no peace.

She thought that, perhaps by taking away the breach between a picture and feeling, she could somehow bring roadkill back to life and might have managed to make more closeness somewhere else, between other best friends. Maybe attending to *elsewhere* is all that you can do when there is not yet a solution for here.

Alone in the street, she burns many pictures that indicate animal violence. When the last picture is burned, a plump form floats down and rests on the ash pile that is stacked in front of her. She picks it up with her hand.

It is not until she makes her way back inside her tiny apartment that she sees that what floated in is in fact a large hawk feather—adding warmth to this warning that is taking over her lonely heart.

LIFE AND DEATH 2

A priestess is licking animal blood from her hands. It is obvious that she is not doing this simply to remove the blood, but for the sake of a strange and befitting ecstasy. She needs the blood. It is unclear, when peering at her, if she has somehow gotten this blood on her hands by handling a shaking shape, or if the blood is actually coming from cuts in her own skin.

In one moment the surrounding trees' leaves burst from green to yellow to red to empurpled mauve to gray.

"Conscious animates are chrism files," she nods, feeling spasms in her body. Fumbling in rare and tumbling epithets, she is a never-ending stitch, an appellation that hopes to finally die having been recognized as someone who literally stands for fusion instead of fracture.

ANOMALY

Alongside the officer's shaming look and tone, the numerous dead rabbits were being gathered by rough hands wearing plastic gloves. The rabbits were being sent from where they had been resting in her freezer to the crime lab for animals. Though she was not the least bit worried about what might come of this situation (in regard to her), she was worried about the interruption of her resting ones. Would the crime lab be the right temperature for her dears to continue resting? Though they might find her fingerprints all over their soft forms, they would not find her fingerprints wrapped around the small necks of the soft ones. She had never murdered anyone, let alone her furry dears. They were like children or friends to her: airy wisps.

They had simply died on certain days when she had been forced to leave the house to go buy more carrots, which, in her opinion, was not technically when her bunnies were even in her care. "How can you be held responsible for caring for something when you are not even there? I was trying to care, by buying them food. Don't you understand?" she hissed toward the officer whom she felt had been implying that there was something wrong with her. Oh no, this was not a misstep. She was apt: making her choices.

Who could blame her for not being able to just throw the lifeless bodies into the trash after they had died? What: should she have put them into the dish disposal? Gotten rid of the evidence of their existence? No! She could never! To have performed a mass burial in her front yard, well, that would have alerted the public, who, in turn, would probably have alerted the cops and she did not need these asshole officers in her home, moving her items this way and that, describing her home with words that hurt her feelings, heads nodding while they probed: "Hoarder hoarder."

She felt it was totally appropriate that, as a manner of protest, she was the one secretly opening various doors to let the rabbits burrow more deeply into hiding places each and every time the officers turned their heads.

They have her cuffed, now. She won't answer their questions until they ask her the right ones: done deal. If they never show her the respect of asking what they ask in ways that honor her experience, then they will be forced to never know that it all started on that loaded day when she could not get the blood of that roadkill bunny off of her favorite apron. When she saw its half-dead form there, squirming in the middle of the road, she needed to get right up close to it: use the cloth of her own life as linen to drape over tender ruin.

BEAR MEDICINE

The shaman had been taking part in Osha digs for many years. It was getting harder to explain shamanist identities as the cities grew and the neighborhoods took over open space, but the urban shaman pressed on and into Earth, considering penetrations of Earth a type of sex in which they had to show utmost care. The shaman felt that now, more than ever, ancient forms of healing by extracting from Earth (and giving back to Earth during that extraction) were needed.

In the digging for Osha, hands are the only tools used. Rattles must be shaking at the side of the generous penetration. Bear-like growls are to be made over the pit as it gets more round and deep, as the soft and pungent root that exists at its base comes closer to the surface, to the face of the one digging. An altar is a place to call home. Once you have freed the base of the root, press the rattle to the ear, call out in mouthed and whispered syllables as you dial somewhere out there to where the bearded grandmothers are leaning over the lip, treating your form as something to interpret.

It is possible to mate spectrally. Do so: mate with your guides.

Familiar with the robust root, its automation of lube-like essence in the human lungs, the shaman closes their eyes. Within them they make the mirror grow gore. They bring the unseen semblances—those invisible silhouettes of wrinkled women—forward. They are what (besides tears) to pour into the open and moist hole where the root waits to be taken to its new home.

Once here in process, the root can't be gotten out any other way than by rocking it. Take up the round with your entire form: improvise the spirit of a circle as a spirited exercise of will.

Bear Medicine 2

On the afternoon of the shaman's death the attendees of the passing ritual tossed the Osha roots (by which they had been gifted with much medicine over the years) into the ground over the dead body. Osha had been too commercially wrought over the recently preceding years for it to be harvested by hand anymore.

When the shaman found out that they could not connect with their root by their hands anymore, that was the first moment when the first things inside of them began to die. The roots that were being tossed in over the dead shaman's body were the last of their kind.

As the roots struck the shaman's body gently, the bodies of a few local bears (that had been "legally hunted" and were dying in the surrounding forest) began to quiver. Jolts shot through them and an overwhelming aroma of flesh, death, and Osha filled the surrounding sky, darkening it completely for a raw moment.

CAVE PEARLS

When he got the email alert and discovered that he had the opportunity to do a cave tour of Son Doong Cave, he spent the remainder of his measly savings account on a one-way ticket to Vietnam. He did not tell his friends so, but his plan was to go into the cave, somehow separate himself from the tour group, find the lake-area in the cave (the place in the cave with no living things in it) and strip down bare before submerging himself into that water as an unconditional promise: a welling finally having made its way up inside of him at the same time as it surrounded.

Cave pearls are made from years of water running too fiercely through a certain area for a stalagmite to appear there. He understood the physiology of cave pearls as dependent on force and duration: knew they could be read as an alternate to him feeling crazed with the dynamisms of his own unfulfilled want.

He had long desired to be anally penetrated by a female lover. He had gone through his life asking for it from some, feeling ashamed of it and hiding it with others, and entirely unmet in his need. That longstanding yearning was just one more bullet point to be added to his bucket list, so much of which would remain unfulfilled upon his death.

No matter how much of his will he put into it he could not fuck himself in the ass and experience fulfillment. He had tried and tried! Look behind the piece of cloth on the top shelf in his bedroom: every shape and size of dildo. Throughout his experimentation, he had to get comfortable with the fact that his need was dependent on *her*: the invisible woman, the woman who never showed up. For him it was as much about the *who* and the *how* as it was about the *what*. Due to his experiences, he had come to realize that he needed to understand his own capacity to bring himself to an infinite cave as the liquid: as force enough to meet and level out a stalagmite-compulsion.

If exposed to air, then cave pearls can appear rougher than they appear to be in the case of a constancy of liquid. A force of liquid penetration by covering keeps the pearls shiny. He understood this as a phenomenon that he did not know how to materialize in his bedroom, his life. He could no longer wait to be tiered and topped by a rarefied female cock: one that flourished from the ground up rather than from the top down (as is the case with a patriarch's cock). In his case, a hearty female, yielding a stalagmite cock, had plainly never made her way to him. So many years of tired and lonesome waiting.

He wanted now to go down as a shiny elemental alongside ages-old and powerful platelets of the deep.

Never recant the incantatory web.

In the dark he is calling out a phantom name, fumbling along the lake's edge in the interior of the infinite cave. He notices that even in a cave full of dark or a world full of darkness, dark can be experienced as decadence.

He feels some tranquility begin to come to him; if he could not be penetrated by a woman with a stalagmite cock in this life, then he certainly didn't want bauble or bullshit. In place of that, he wished to die with his hands and mouth and anus full of muddy pearls: mala beads sliding into him one knob at a time until they exited him through a topmost gland, a chakra that he was finally enabled to foster: his crown.

WETNESS FOR WITNESS

Each time she woke, she felt strongly that the wetness could not be helped; the wetness that dripped freely down her legs felt like a turned-on faucet. It was directly credited to some form of intergalactic lubrication. The space of visions and dreams had always made her wet. Each time she dreamt of the sharp edges of collages, the floods would come in and drown the pocket between her thighs.

As she aged she came to know that this wetness was different than the wetness that happened with lovers. Unlike the case with lovers (where she needed lube to be given her in order for her to proceed comfortably in her body), here, between vision and awake, she was getting lube from her body.

Daily she continued to travel to the sea's edge. This was the place to beat out her trials, her throbbing, the places in her that felt shunted or discontinued by being forced into a waking state. She had long chosen out of Western medicine as a way of choosing more fully into this place whereby she thrashes and releases tears indiscernible from the salty, moving rush, the brash tides outside her window.

Wetness is for this: finding edges in the yoke and then staying with them, courting them to release.

Copulatory Lock

Sexual intimidation doesn't happen in Hyena culture. If it's not consensual then it simply is not: end of discussion.

Based on the location of her masculinized genitalia (shaped like a penis, but hanging flaccid between her legs) he literally has to squat and dance behind her, moving into her squat, in order to even penetrate her penis with his. Her sexual center is pointing ahead: his follows from behind, into her and through her to the degree that she wants it. She is the stipulation here. She is his direction.

Aware that some gymnastics are required in order for mating to occur, if the female is keen on him, *she* will lead *him* up the hill or out to the brink where there is the most likelihood for safe copulation. He follows her to their spot. At the moment of intromission the hyena's bodies literally lock in order for exchange to occur. This locking makes fruition and impregnation possible at the same moment that it dramatically increases the risk of the two being seen as a lager body of flesh and then eaten with excitement: a predator's conglomerate meat.

As the lion nears he does not have a choice. His hormones are raging in response to their hormones raging. With *doubled flesh* before him, he rushes the magic to feast on something more integrated than yin and yang. Yin and yang have that curved line between them, indicating their difference. The hyenas' copulatory lock means, in her choosing to let him, they have found their way beyond the line.

TIME

So much about how quotidian hours feel had always felt wrong to xem: stuttering enforcements, abrupt amputations of psychic realms as soon as someone turned the cubicle corner, gems being robbed of their glistening as a flip of the calendar took place.

Because of xyr embodied refusal of the notion of quotidian hours as the primary force driving existence, xe collected hourglasses: piles of them. "Better to express the present as between something and something else, since the only times I have ever felt time as something other than injury have been when I am between this time and that time."

The notion of time as a flatness barreling itself through you like innumerable and untraceable particles of sand, which, as they pass, take some of you with them, drain out of the form never to return, give none of you back to yourself, was utterly absurd to xem. Xe pondered this, considered how to thwart it.

In xyr ritual act of upbraiding, xe would definitely taste the salt, drown on xyr tears which operate as such contrast to the sand that leaves. In xyr ritual acts xe could feel quotidian hours as mere limits, illusions, flaws.

Xe preferred to not perch in something to which xe never agreed. Therefore, xe piled tear-shaped glass orbs that share middles and xe piled them in an anonymous field.

Xe put on xyr best pair of boots to smash this: body-skills capable of killing time.

FIRE AND MIST

For Max Regan

Every book he has ever written possesses a title that relates to fire. Blood-red content is a way to burst open a bodice; is the story of picking up her single earring off of the floor or hanging her crumpled dress on the bedroom door after they make love and she scampers off to use the bathroom. His relationship to lyric comes from the way that he has personally vowed to touch her body: tender flame to replace what terseness or arson she has ever been subjected to in the past.

He is inflamed by women and wads: sensuous adduction. Posit is built into his gender. Extended, he postures as he leads her from here to there with a bounce in his step. By rolling the newspaper in hand he makes a flower-shape for her: "Voilà! Abiogenesis!" He hands her his idea of a parasitic portrait: a cliché that remains beautiful as it moistens and decays in the winter weather. She loves him. She plans to someday offer him the wad-flower that he has made for her: something else for him to burn. She sees his gelatin swagger as fire being held up to a mirror.

He breathes in the clarity of a winter morning not unlike many others. He remembers the chimney that he saw surrounded by mist. He had been traveling, and to him, that chimney was a stalwart singularity hinting at where abrupt erections warm. Replicating the argument (that he had recently had with his buddy) again in his mind, he still feels that mist on all sides of you is a valid approach to human direction. North, South, East and West are not all that there is.

He remembers how his tears hissed when they fell on the Sarcode's spears in front of him as he gawked at the chimney being slowly ravaged by the snow. He wanted a her then. He had not yet found her. Oregon's Snow Flowers are intensity-ensuring mutualisms, and he did not know what they were when he first experienced them.

As he is walking up the street a few blocks from his apartment, he sees thick smoke hurling up out of the top of a building. He won't know until he gets closer to home that his books and his lover's dress have been burned to ash in the house fire. All that is left is the implication of a structural framework of what was once a house.

Even in his grief he is holding her. She hugs him firmly to her, too. She reminds him that not all bareness need be seen as destruction. It's about how you read a moment, she thinks: "There is a chimney in a different state that has always meant awe to you." No need for a surrounding house if you have a chimney with mystical ash in it.

Handing him her copy of his book (since he no longer has a copy of his own book, all of them burned in the fire) she jumps on the back of his motorcycle and leans into him, urging him to take them on their way. Her warmth causes his skin to relax. His breath releases. They go toward the mist.

HORNS

For Samuel Ace

Turning the awareness of anomalies into a community *of* anomalies proves that anomalies are not something far off. They are each one of us and if it is one it is always more than one.

She has been wrestling with them her whole life. There is only conjecture as to their cause. She has two while others have one protruding from the middle of their forehead. As a child, she is called devil. In high school she tries to cut them off with her own razor. She fixates. She saws and saws with her eyes wide open until there is blood in her hair. She worries about them showing. When she is cutting them off she does not even remember to shave her legs.

She learns, much later on in life, that her horns could have come up through skin vulnerabilities, scarring from the burns of fires. She has never experienced being physically burned by a fire, though she often dreams of girls screaming and nodding their heads wildly, emitting flames in a voluptuous yes, as they run toward and project themselves into damp vats of salt and hair: hot englut, temperature as a way to clot wetness.

In her thirties she meets him. She feels lucky to have. He is a trans man, knows what it is like to have a body with which one cannot identify without things being done to that body. When he fucks her he often places his hand between her horns, but only after she invites him in: his dick between her legs. He applies pressure on the top of her head. He can see gold penetrate through her skull, past the skin that keeps her brain and thoughts and insecurities inside of her.

Though she won't let him stroke them during sex, sometimes, when they are together in the room at night, in the dark, she will bring his hand ever so slowly toward the top of her head. Once it reaches them, she moves him over her with affectionate hands. That makes the most sense to her: just like she moves her hands over his dick when the time is right.

KIVA WORSHIP

The sacred question and the sacred answer are the same spiritual essence: solid essence, a salt-lick, a chunk of amber, dark light.

Dark light tends toward tenderness and tenderness loosens the cells enough for deific onslaught to take place. There are infinite hymens for breaking, infinite immanent-yet-dependent identities of moments in which to animate. Handle Gaia with chivalry and care. Self-inseminate on behalf of overtones, on behalf of patterns able to be reared.

Internal altar provides fathomless fodder.

What can be heard of the soul in a homespun realm? We want our memories to be able to have minds of their own: be imbued with the spiritual livelihood of reach. Sounds catch on rounded walls, on round arms and round legs. We squat to be perceived as stout, close to the ground. We are practitioners who know how to work with visions of different sizes and shapes of crops. Corn unlocks us: corn is both cunt and cock.

Harmonic in our intent, we are always able to bring forth more rain than was predicted. We pray until the kiva fills with flood-water and our tears and groans combine. When practicing in an underground womb, while there is such thing as too much sunlight ("please pull up the ladder and close the hatch!") there can never be too much husky glow.

MEMOIR RECALLS

Wanting her life to come off as having somehow curved itself, she began writing her memoir at age thirteen. She wanted to give her experiences the chance to grow along with her, wrap around her. She wanted to work the necessary asphyxiations and the necessary surrogacies in order that they enable unexpected refinement in her. She planned to write her memoir as a synesthetic plot: something that goes on in many different directions of her for the duration of her.

She needed the form in which she wrote to evolve along with a continuity of her coming of age by trance. Trance means traveling, but without your mind as it usually functions. She believed that, through her work, her memories could eventually have a mind of their own. Flirting with cliché, she took personally what happened when it softened and became vulnerable to her voice: touch-butter, a way for her to tell her stories.

Perform the complexities you create. Track the molecules of an ongoing beast-fable. Douse in sentences; dowse for sentences as rotund extremes.

The Banyan tree's roots are moving upward and its branches downward: aspects reaching inversely. She wonders on the form of her memoir as an inverse-universal, a startling epiphyte: mutual turning and traction in which miracles can be expressed. It flourishes by what first seems like embellishment. In the flourish, it then slowly strangles what was, eventually leaving its beginning hollow, able to move on.

Amiss and Amok

The Venus of Willendorf is plagued with a peculiar but befitting dysphoria. Afraid of her aesthetic shifts ever being misread by others, ever being used as cultural stigma in support of any form of reductiveness, she is impassioned to emphasize, "Nothing in these shifts, nothing in this weight change, this weight loss, is indicative of anything lost."

She is not trying to lose weight. She has just been more into root vegetables lately. Her weight loss is not meant to be a message or a future measure regarding the female form for generations to come. Her body is not something to be used to make a point. Her hands grab her own belly-fat with a ferociousness that is familiar with itself. She is a living state; she is the summation of her skills at work to elaborate bulk.

She pulls her belly-fat out toward you and states, "I am still here for you in the same ways I have always been. The path clots, congeals in certain areas before shrinking a bit and settling back into itself again." Fluctuations of the body are its valor. The drama in which to attend and attune is the enlivening and making-more-subtle of the body before it becomes entirely stone.

"Do you realize I can't stand up on my own? There is no upward state for me without you in me, relating to me accurately. I depend on your hands wrapped around me as you keep me upright while taking me with you into battle as a reminder. Transition is heavy. Any misinterpretation of me could very well be the death of me, could cause me to crumble in your hand.

Regardless of what is seen as happening on the level of my physical form, I remain an extreme: indelible obesity. Revel in that fact in your third eye, please, if what your human eyes relay is confusing to you. I would rather have you see me with your eyes closed than to have you misread me.

The carnivorous voles are running and squealing in the expanse as additives to the undersides of my slow-moving gait. This is a performance of unconditional obeisance. Add to me and be with me. Together we will increase, amok."

A Jetty at Low Tide Leads

In its emergence it always led us to the place both mythic and true. The ephemeral bridge was the cause, enabling a spillway-sacrament: life in alignment, anointing while announcement was taking place.

We have been drawing the blue moons of The Lady of the Lake on our children's foreheads for years: boys and girls both. We believe this will enable them to become themselves. Teaching them by modeling, we run our hands through the surface of the water, making small waves within what is being reflected back to us. In doing so, we disturb seemingly stopped or pent-up reflections. The waves within the reflection emphasize the importance of keeping the body soft.

This *soft* is not some limit, based in socialized femininity. It is the softness of priests and priestesses for centuries, in devotion to the mists and fog, to subliminal voices adjusting octaves over time. For us, it is really about keeping the joints and hinges nimble, limber, lubed, so that at any moment our bodies can be an ephemeral bridge for her should she need that of any one of us.

There are rhythms in the reflection. How can we live by these if we do not seek them by intensifying and dissipating alongside, within, by way of?

We keep the mirror moving in order to keep the dream microbes from being murdered.

DAY OF THE DEAD

When you come to what you perceive to be the end of a picture or an identity, don't stop there. Instead, project onto it as indicative of need for a new beginning to be brought forth. At that site of elegant twist, reverently open a death. To do so will please them.

When I was a child, instead of trying to dismember or disembowel dolls, I would always bring dolls into dark streams in the room as if I were a pioneer for finding suitable places for them to fuck. In the passion-thesis, several things must occur: intentional increase of molecular awareness, relentless grip of the radiating bone.

When you are the aide of an edge it is your responsibility to change the altar. It is customary to adorn the space of amorous exultation with *their* most prized possessions. In this context of worship, they don't need your stuff, they need *you*; you can leave your prizes at home.

A skeleton made of gossamer threads slowly makes its way from below, upward. It is going to burst through the floor.

You and your fellow practitioners feel an inner urgency to respond by performing incubation-theater: bringing in red leaves and keeping them on the temple floor for several days until they have yellowed. All of you hope that the yellow leaves, if left for an additional time after the celebration, will miraculously progress into something else.

Your face is painted with edible colors, shapes that hint, odiferous doors. You lick your lips all the way to your cheeks as you stretch out your mouth and envision your entangled dolls preparing to speak. By putting the radiating bone between your legs like an erection, you free up space in both of your hands; with an ornamented skull in each hand you publicly thank the ancestors for offering you new skills.

You repeat to fellow practitioners what the ancestors have emphasized to you: "Regardless of what others may profess, with whom you merge are not only near during this one time of the year." They have repeatedly impressed on you to look upon the pine trees which surround the temple; these are the pine trees from which the temple was built so long ago, and pine is not deciduous; it doesn't change its face and it will never grimace at you. It will emote along with you, forever.

The ancestors are so often ahead of schedule. Even though they have already died, they are ahead of their time. The verdures on the temple floor suddenly, violently materialize as something radical: plump, clean pages from the detritus of intentionally placed fallen leaves.

ENCODED WITHIN THE AKASHIK RECORDS

Are your wings animal, mineral or angel?

Stellular.

Stellular pictures keep the third eye in constant use, in calisthenics. This is the composition of immeasurable circuitry: adding until laden. If you are the one inducing it, is a visitation a visitation? Are there types of visitation that are a direct result of embodied volition? The contrary questions that hover just outside of an answer's view are information encoded in aether.

Aether: cuneiform skin-script that keeps Avalon, Atlantis, Lemuria and other mysterious areas clandestine to the human eye.

Xe had spent a long time working with the backsides, reverses and flip-sides of deities. Xe was beginning to feel like it was about time xe initiated working with them face to face. A gelatinous fractal magnetizes a body into elasticity, into ecstasies. This form of primordial beauty is not debatable.

Face to face, xe transfers the archetype of the martyr into the archetype of the healer. Earth, air, fire and water are all called upon in the process. Xe makes enigmatic inscriptions in sound-densities. Xe perceives the entire field of plants as stuffed with numen.

CHAKRA AUTOBIOGRAPHY OF A DEIFIC HER

Nude men kneel before her without shame. Their ritual objects are full for her, full of her. The hair that has fallen from her head has been collected by them. Where they have placed it in their ritual objects, it floats. She peers into the contents within what it is that these men bear and she sees her own reflection floating on the quality of their sacrifice. They love her reflection almost as much as she does. By putting gender back into the human body as mystery, outside of time, the whole group of them is releasing gender from threat of patriarchal disambiguation.

Inanna's reasoning for visiting the Underworld was a blurred one. Those who worshipped her did not understand her choice. They felt the fur that had grown around them to hold them into her beginning to split. The animality meant to seal them irrevocably into her fertility was coming undone due to her own desire to affect the design.

Clots and altars had always been her favorite kinds of nature. She resonated with paradox, too. Inanna passed through the seven gates, all the while losing aspects of her garb, having her ritual objects and ultimately her scepter taken from her: facets removed from her identity, curves becoming distant from her portrait.

The Goddess's body, bleeding and lifeless on a gleaming meat-hook, shakes the land below it. Below is where she hangs. Upon Inanna's death, nature died with her. The grass beneath the feet of the nude men became instantly dry before inverting, burrowing down below the surface soil.

The way that she had harvested their masculinity (in ways that allowed them to remain soft), was suddenly absent. Their deportment shifted. They dropped their ritual objects and picked up sticks, posturing to use them as swords on one another. They felt their bodies creak and crack. Their identities, once used to reify fertility, were now leaking out of containments. They covered themselves in leaves soaked in one another's blood, refused to be nude anymore. Nude men can't perform for the Goddess of fertility without being entangled in her stare.

In the Otherworld of her death, Inanna was seeing herself without a reflection. In the void, she was tying knots between hair fallen out of her head and hair that hung from her head on the day that she died. When alive, she had struggled so with all notions of a separate sense of self: "I am not me to myself without another's body inside of that sense of self."

It is one's right as a practitioner to do psychic surgery on oneself in any moment, to do so for the sake of enabling cell-merge. But what was she trying to link up? What was she in need of looking up to? What was out of place in her chakra autobiography?

Sadhu?

He suddenly left his training.

Granted, it was not formal training. There was certainly no clique of which he was a part, no guaranteed group from which he could draw support. The point of his practice was to move his body to the fringes, and then to turn his body into a fringe on which he could practice, regardless of exterior circumstance. This is how the ashram becomes an internal fact. This is the cemetery as a sacred-site for unforeseen forms of flourish.

To commit oneself each day at the plump belly of the Ganges, and to do so via the saffron and vermillion-colored vestments and the weighty renunciations, meant that he had committed to training *himself*.

Forced by exterior circumstance to put on a suit and tie, he boarded the plane.

Regardless of his migration, he continued to mouth his mantra, internally: sometimes aloud, too. Daily, he intentionally remembered attending his own funeral. Being considered legally dead to himself and his country, he decided he could possibly bring himself back to life in a new way upon this forced geographical shift: living in America.

"There are many different ways to perform your form," he tells himself. To others he is talking to himself, but to him, he is reciting: "I still have this fragment of my guru's skull. I will keep it close and in that, he will keep me close."

Twenty years later, while meandering in the thrift store, still moaning his mantra with as much regularity as he would have had he stayed in his birth country, he finds three ninety-nine-cent apothecary bottles filled with bright spices. He breaks down weeping, right there in the store. He grips the sliver of bone tight, piercing his ruddy hand.

His tears call out to Shiva, right there in the aisle.

DISCONNECT

She is thinking about accidentals in music. She ponders how, by semitone, accidentals put a bend in the form at hand, cause it to sink below itself. Accidentals are a stimulating part of the music because they do not fit in the scale. She recalls how they are an integral part of Gregorian chant: the type of music from which the flat sign and sharp sign emerged.

While applying acne medicine to her own face she counts every role for which she has auditioned and not been chosen. For so long she had thought that it was some issue with her voice, how it sounded, her pitch, but with the recent card that she had gotten from the director (for whom she had just auditioned) informing her that her "voice was astounding and unique," but they "could not work with what she looked like," she had, now, for the first time, allowed herself to think back on her past: grieve the missed sounds and operatic stories of which she could not be a part simply because of something that had nothing to do with her. Her acne was not her fault!

Her day job was a let-down. It was pretty easy: too easy for her. And, beyond that, she was not allowed to sing in the thrift store: told by her boss that it "might make the customers uncomfortable." Her day job left her with a lot of time to ponder injustice and accidentals.

When she saw the man with the three spice-filled apothecary bottles coming slowly up to her register, she felt a sudden lift in her spirit. "He's probably not from here. Finally, maybe I will be able to be around someone who can see me for *who I am*." Hearing him talk about spices and those glass bottles with their corks, they had almost gotten entirely through the transaction when, seemingly out of nowhere, he made a comment about a certain kind of spice that could be crushed up and applied to her face. "That acne will clear right up."

Her heart descended from where it previously was in her body. The weight of the wound caused the whole room to quiver off-balance.

DEATH AS SYNTHESIS

It is a terrible feeling to accidentally bruise your fruit. You respond to your accidents by intercession, with infusions that add more expectation to the ethics by which you continue.

Xe is pulling at the layer of chainmail under xyr skin. This causes xyr skin to bleed.

Ever since the first time contact was made with a flying bird, xe has carried around a chainmail swatch large enough to cover a condor's body, wings and all. Xe cannot explain why, while riding xyr bike, birds regularly fly directly into xyr bike or body: from getting caught in the bike spokes to smacking directly into xyr face. Bloodying beak.

"Due to them making themselves present, I relate as much to the sounds gathering and protruding from the undersides of flying birds as I do to the birds themselves. The sounds are how I know they are coming for me, coming to strike, to collaborate impact."

Xe is becoming more aware that wholeness is xyr right and that a somatic sense of wholeness does not happen without sound and the requirement of xyr effort.

There's always more silage when xe returns to the aberration.

SOUND

The reckoning: while hearing is one of the five senses, sound is a sense-making wizard. Sound is precise lube: tenderizing accompaniment to downloads from dark matter.

As a shaman I shake until I am all shale: shake until there is no more ignominy. Wrought particles emerge as figures with carnivorous hearts: blood-Edens chomping on themselves. This is a way to unearth viscera. Wooden roots are being razed. Inner riots ensue as a form of varnish.

Intuitive literature is a new Gaia-elemental. Pages are a way to cosmically commune.

The dark mother: burning in a perpetually bearded place.

Linen-Limen

There are so many ways to open the gates. Doing so fleshes out the remaining parts of one's fate, the parts that have ever been flushed out or made limp by another's berate.

Since xe was a teenager xe had always packed. What xe packed, however, was not a singularity but in rotary. From shoving stockings, stuffed animals and small figurines between xyr legs, as a child, to the teenage evolution into working with a strap-on or a perfectly cock-like glass vegetable or sometimes even a cloth-cock-wad of bulky linen, xe identified with everything with which xe packed. Conversely hard and then soft, they all felt the same to xem when xe knelt slowly, moving the orgy of energy during practice of tai chi.

"The work is to find agency as a fondness in the trigger," xe whispers with a bit of a moan while moving. Gender for xem was like learning to keep xyr eyes closed as a place wherein agency could be unconditionally infused, while xyr eyes were literally open in a room. This way there would be no distractions, and xyr involvement could be unconditional and consistent: coaxing the cloaca, magnifying where shade is a quality of space, a place ridden with ephemeral seeds.

It's not that xe was cocky. It's that confidence is inborn-bridge and xe reserved the right to always still have something to learn about what it is that xe was embodying, as declaration with blaring confidence as xe was declaring it. "I knowingly keep mystery in my form."

Signage enables. Fields of flowers become moist pillowcases and bushy ribbons combusting into flame. "I stain fabric with my essences because fabric really does retain me! My cloth-cock is a part of the tiers of my cock."

Lean your entire body weight into your front. Make a crease

there. Then, lay the whole of the weight of your third eye back, and into your hood. When you shove yourself against it, it becomes a flocculent bowl to hold your flow.

ELK

During the process, it was not that she was trying to gain weight, though she certainly was not focused on losing it. Her inner feeling was that, in attempting to write her memoir, her personal fables were gaining such ground within her, getting so large, that they were literally stretching out her body.

Before ever making them into pages she had spent years cross-fertilizing the tales within. She related to a premise that page could be literal action, not just narration. With the same hands that she planned, one day, to use to write the fables of her body as pages, she would constantly ink the stretch marks, add kohl-color in the leaky lines which indicated that she was growing, making her way by nature from a young buck to an elder.

During one, cold, winter afternoon she went to put on her cape. It did not fit her body anymore. She cut the gray fabric up the side so she would be able to continue wearing it regardless of whether or not it fit her. "That makes sense for my stories too," she thought. "The pages have to be expansive enough to appropriately house rogue elegance and essence."

Then, on the trail, in her demeanor and mood, she was penetrated: antler lengths coming up from the soil and shocking between her legs, antler tips ramming into her third eye. "The pages need to express this as well: shocking blares, textures."

The contrast of the two revelations made her feel more skilled about the contexts of her own pages, but also left her desperately in need of an elk's velvet hide in which to wrap herself: in which to be wrapped by another.

Witness to the full-grown elk, she was instantaneously made an observer of subtle dynamism ushering her by rite into immortal portico.

DEFENSIVE

He knew that he was with a powerhouse woman. He sometimes called her that when talking to his friends. He respected her from the moment he met her: the moment in which she was cussing out a parent for cussing at their children. He wanted her to feel how powerful he knew her to be as she became honed.

Both of them were intimately involved in their own spirit and body mantras. Due to this, they found that at many times in their relationship they were overcome with union and alignments: awe-based projections of the Beloved of whom mystics had long written. They also realized that there were times in experience in which grave separations overtook them: nearly no ability to knit closeness between.

During one such somatic storm, she was yelling at the top of her lungs, yanking at her hair. He was late tonight and she had started bleeding. He had been attending consecutive week-long retreats during which time laundry and dishes were piling up around the house. Whether or not he was being schooled in shamanic travel, she needed more of him. Had he gotten his roots all tied up: fallen in love with another woman or some guru? There was disjunction.

Meanwhile, he had been having a hard time finding his way back here when traveling astrally. He would wake from said travels with hundreds of bruises all over his body, even though, during the travel, the physical body never moved from where it began: right there on the carpet in the dark room.

How had he gotten these? What were they indicating?

Bruises in unexplainable places.

When he got home, she started yelling, put pressure on him until he gave in: began to confess content, the cause of the bruises. Though he actually had no memory of how they had been acquired he found it good to defend the secret inner-life of the bruise, even if that required that he make some narrative up out of intuition or even thin air.

DIPLOGENESIS

She was anchored to perpetuating contexts by which the double monster could develop: come to be loved by another side of its pair. She lived by doubling dynamisms as constant inspiration, as a carving tool, as a map for additivity.

Profound inductions of magnetism without linearity.

The bearded mother has always had a double womb. In it, a fetus doubles, its forthcoming signature becomes encumbered, its decay and animations lodge in pomosexual cause. A cave is a womb that can be wrapped around someone's warps, a room in which the bearded mother can cover a her with an infinity of layers: the jangling weight of capes and robes draped over her one by one.

Having long been a lover of women, she struggled more with calling herself a lesbian than she ever did with loving and fucking women. Somehow she felt that the term did not connote a vast enough span for the needed doubling. Is "lesbian" a limiting directionality of loving? What of the other sides?

She felt it to be her memory of herself as a cell of the swain-Goddess (that bearded mother) which caused her to incessantly dream of herself bearing men's hands.

Real Faux

For Julieanne Combest

Never avoid the incentive to shape-shift alongside a current flow. You don't have to pronate gyration. It's not necessary to enforce yourself as something second to one already extant. Let this complete its current turn, keep you as spin within it.

My phallus-shaped candle isn't the only one that did not fit in the candelabra. The carnage of pronouns is pushing itself through, discerning itself as implacable. Our bodies are being turned into rue: the long-laden collaboration.

Just like we never wash our hands after sex with our lovers, we must keep our own tears close to us. They are precursor to the temple not yet built. Tears are the place in which we dance the chakras while we are instigating sanctified breathing: soft walls in which we will dance ourselves in the future.

We knowingly and actively project collaboration onto moments because to do so could enable poise, could dissuade slumping and fatigue. By energetically imbuing moments, moments might actually begin to react in support of us.

In the near future, a temple will be built as a reifying of our main. This must be done, because no temple in which to share course and pour means no foaming home for so much monthly bleeding.

Real monks who wear both real and faux mink.

Mink-monks: a constant need to willfully compose catharsis.

REAL IDENTITY

It was not his pages that made him identify as a poet.

Sure, publishers had classified his writing as poetry on Amazon and at Small Press Distribution, but he had also been known to posit to publishers that he did not classify himself in the ways that they classified him. He preferred to perceive his books as unique beasts: breasted, yeasty, phallic and untamable.

When he began walking the neighborhood streets with his knife, intending to cut down all of the shoes with those tied laces weighing down the power lines, he thought, for a moment, that he might be becoming a poet. This felt like poetic act to him. Attuning to the sense of walking in the shoes of someone murdered in a turf war made him feel all that was awry in his own body, possibly even his identity.

Compelled to work the amiss into memoir, to tell the stories of shocks in autobiography form as poetic act, he was gaining a psychic credential.

The real identities: not false but able to be argued by another as fiction.

SANCTIFIED SPACE IS FOR SCARIFICATION

Ritual sex with ephemera is a way to hypostatize totems as inebriations integral to the sexuality at hand. Our group of practicing priestesses feels ourselves being subjected to mediation of spiritual power as a public sexuality: mysterious force turning us into cosmic subject.

It's not precisely that our genitals or our identities are in our hands, right now, as we are speaking. It is the case, however, that this group of us has gathered together to provide support to one another as we continue to pump large crystals through the pores of our hearts. Some of us see the crystals as protuberant, dick-shaped. Others of us see the crystals we birth as opaque and luminous: shapes but not distinct shapes. Others of us envision what we push through as merciful approximations to the yoni.

It is not solely how we identify with our own as much as it is our own and how we identify with another. This is where the mystical masculine enters. This masculinity is made in secret forests like herbs are: masculinity made in the complexities of the queer body and not in the mouth of some patriarch for whom control of a queer's body is priority.

Rituals for the individual must be made. If an entire temple exists simply for an integral, individual ritual to take place, the temple will have fulfilled its purpose. One of us dips their hands in red, liquid wax at the threshold crossing. The heat of the wax burns the body, causes the priestess to scream and the sound comes out as rhythm and cream. This priestess needs this quality of intensity in order for her cells to retain.

Another writes in red ink on decaying pink petals. They do it over in the corner, when everyone else has gone home, when no one but the temple is watching. For them, the way the letters imprint the actual materiality of the petals, simulacrum to their own volition causing corrosion in nature, reminds them of elemental power. "The human is only as far apart from nature as we choose to be," they grunt.

We never agreed to what we inherited: the threads of recollection having been cut before we could even lean into them and be held by what is rightfully ours. Adhering to the most personal of particulars gives us leverage: a lyrical strength. We come here to reminisce, to collide, to teach ourselves (and each other) how to soften at will.

From Within

From within a constant twilight of her own creation she practiced seeing dreams as the bardos present just after death: dreams as hooded, holding epochs.

Opening and closing her eyes while dreaming, sometimes she followed the light by choice; other times, she let herself intentionally get caught, be flooded to a cliff's edge or dropped into a bog or some peculiar, infinitely dark bag. For the sake of knowing personally a particular emanation within a bedrock of emanations, she wanted to see what she was able to accomplish when the ions were drenched with tendency toward inundation. Resolve inundation or add to it? There is agency to be felt in dream states, in bardos.

Her very first dream was of the epiphany of cherubs who possessed what she perceived to be overweight genitals protruding from their perinea: smoky, leaky, angel-claws. As the cherubs flew, sinking a bit in the moon-soaked night air due to the weight of those claws and what they were destined to carry, she sensed that the genitals of these cherubs were archives for her.

Enthrall is enthroning: eccentric accentuations being sensed in the darkest times of night.

HOOK

As her lover adjusted their fingers inside of her she felt something within her shape-shifting.

It was all beginning to resemble a hook. This felt so right, physically: arousing but also somehow cosmically relaxing. The image of her identity was insistently loosening from inside of her. More and more able to open, she was somatically realizing her vagina as a living raptor-talon: a meat-tearing entity. As with the overweight angel-claws (which burned themselves into her as phantasmagorical ideals when she was a child), her vagina was revealing itself as a gripping bird of prey: a place in which animal meat could be torn, prepared to be sacro-magically consumed.

Her lover was a woman, but woman, herein, did not mean that her lover related to their own vagina: they related most to hers. Was her lover's hooked hand a totem for her oncoming orgasm? Was her talon-cunt so active now because it had recently been resting in its essence during the weeks of menstrual bleeding? Do totems for future orgasms enjoy being stored in bowls of milky blood?

Clenching her vaginal talon around her lover was her right: internal talon to unconditionally squeeze her lover's subliminal dick.

FEATHER GENDERS

How best to address eons of aether? By what shape-shifting endeavors might these animate anointers most evolve?

A group of martyrs is collaboratively growing new genders. These genders have feathers. Owl feathers are sprouting out of the tips of fingers and toes, out of spines. By many types of benevolent shaking, the group mutates within their immortality. They decide not to leave mortality, by choosing instead to let in light, breathe hard into chipped goblets, constantly permeate the third eye as an activist-embodiment of *pleroma.*

To keep activism in the physicality of the form guarantees that the activism will always be wet. Ice is gathering on the skins of forms. When haunted by ice, they instruct each other to go inward for the moist, soft hunt: "Go in as a cell-mage; go in for shamanisms of she-gore."

Like stroking black eggplants in the dark, for them, all composition is sex and love as ancient sentiment. So many reoccurences of shadow life have long revealed the cannibalistic caveat: "Cave light is meant to deliver us as quest by which we might step into an even deeper light. Light to lead us to other lights." What light is deeper than cave light?

The single members of the group have managed to find each other. They come into an area together to intentionally forget their past altars. In pursuit of and enrobed in the holy alias, they strive for alternates to their forms being an unquestioned sounding-chamber for cosmic grief.

COLONY COLLAPSE

We were living in the era known for it.

After the last of the bees had died, all of the vegetables dwindled, disappeared. Culture shifted. Folks no longer went out on dates to eat together. Food was no longer treated as something by which pleasure could be experienced. There was too much guilt while eating; there was too much loss.

What was eaten was some sort of mock: a mockery of the planet's primordial relation to and creation of beauty; beauty was inborn to this place before we did this. Now, food tasted like a bad accident: dirty socks, shrunken and artificial approximations filling up too-big plates. It was a regular ritual for people to hold plump and true-to-scale plastic vegetables in their hands like textural prayers while they ate what was incapable of giving them pleasure. These were the prayers to and the grief at loss of what once was.

Bee paralysis happened slowly: not exactly lethal but dramatic enough to impact. Bees would walk when they should have been flying, would lie on their backs and stare into the sun when they should have been walking. Bees would fall off of the edge of the lip of their hive. Bee keepers began to see the visionaries of the hives, their sweet queens, fall over dead on their thrones. When the queen died, the heartbeat of the hive instantly warped. The sound of the workers and drones going into shock at the loss of their queen was a path to the future's dreadful, yet crucial story.

This was not fate; it was during our era that we made our world this way and we were living now, with the weight of our past responsibility going unanswered by us. We thought we were too busy to consider this when we were spraying our gardens. We thought the bees would never leave us. It has taken us time to realize that they, in fact, did not leave us.

It was we who ousted the grandeur of their nature.

197

Outing the Outline in Hopes of Filling in the Silhouette

Sometimes, exhibiting to someone something that they already know increases the grounding that might be shared between the two of you. Touch me in a familiar way so that I can see myself in you, you in me. I need to see what you in me and me in you means for land. That allows me to know that I am land. To be me, from this place, means that I can feel that I belong here. Touch me so that I can recall what has already been retained.

She had been doing this as a way of trying to bring him back to himself (and therefore to her), ever since the vegetables withered away. Day and night she attended his ailment: rubbed piles of glass vegetables all over his skin. An artist had come up with the idea of blowing glass in the shape of carrots, corn, and eggplant to help people remember, to encourage hope.

Suffice it to say, she was actually rubbing him with glass, phallus-shapes capable of reflecting, but she did not need to tell him that. It might distract him from the release that he so needed. The releases on which they both depended in him were no longer targeted at his penis. Now, the releases were inductions: psychic cream moving in between his skin and his organs after such deep massage by a replicated, phallic object.

It was obvious to her how dependent his joy had become on particular Earth elements. Fact: edible vegetables made him feel strong, green. Vegetables made him her Adam. Without them he had no way to access memory of the initial, sacred place that, while it certainly came from her, also came from his body.

She understood it: no matter what happened exteriorly, in the environment, she could always recognize herself as the garden due to the flame which burned green (that flame that she had set loose in her womb long before). Oh Adam-in-a-flicker. Oh demure mirror. Because of her relations to her womb, she had a piece of vision that he just did not have.

Her adamancy that he know himself in the context of what she could bring out of him aligned with their collaborative understanding of the original work in Eden. She liked to push her man, and frankly, she had had years to build up familiarity with how to work with this by means of her own dildo.

Purifications must be carried forth. First, particle-like glass on skin, then, salt water poured over bowls full of phallic, glass shapes.

NEVER ENOUGH

There were not many choices left for them to make: at least, not choices that came from their nature. Most of their nature died with the bees.

They decided it would be so: for the rest of their lives they would collaboratively worship Agni. Even though it was no longer possible for their choices to relate to their nature, they found through practice of a new authenticity, that their choices could reify their nature. They knew, however, that living by such a decision would set them apart from the rest of their species.

It was as if they had gone crazy: they just could not get married enough. They pursued marriages beyond number: each in a different location, with a different set of turgid decorations and accoutrements. They invited another, then another group of sweating attendees. Their marriages brought them closer to the honey, the prismatic memory of the sound that the hive once made. Their marriages brought them *closer*, one ceremony at a time.

They spent all of the money they had accumulated during their work in the corporate world, and they traveled. Their travel was never without mourning. They could feel it all: ground withering, tree boughs on the trees in the Garden of Eden simply falling off, paper in pulp-form clogging streams, desert weeping an azure blue glint hinting at the color of the queen bee's belly.

It got to the point in their process where that was the only thing they ever did anymore: travel and marry. They stopped eating altogether and focused all of the force of their attention on this: the new life that they would live while their bodies withered away: every moment, a wedding.

Publication Credits

Thanks to the following journals and small presses where some of these essays have appeared (or are forthcoming):

Nous-zot Press, Underground Books, Berfrois, Caliban Online, Gone Lawn, Eccolinguistics, MadHat Lit and MadHat Annual, Angelhouse Press and *Momoware.*

About the Author

j/j hastain is a collaborator, writer and maker of things. j/j performs ceremonial gore. Chasing and courting the animate and potentially enlivening decay that exists between seer and singer, j/j, simply, hopes to make the God/dess of stone moan and nod deeply through the waxing and waning seasons of the moon.

j/j hastain is the inventor of The Mystical Sentence Projects and author of several cross-genre books including the trans-genre book *libertine monk* (Scrambler Press), *The Non-Novels* (Spuyten Duyvil), *Luci: a Forbidden Soteriology* (Black Radish Books) and *The Xyr Trilogy: a Metaphysical Romance of Experimental Realisms.* j/j's writing has most recently appeared in *Caketrain, Trickhouse, The Collagist, Housefire, Bombay Gin, Aufgabe* and *Tarpaulin Sky.*

www.ingramcontent.com/pod-product-compliance
Lightning Source LLC
Chambersburg PA
CBHW030518020726
47494CB00004B/1150